Absolutely Nothing
to Get Alarmed About

BY CHARLES WRIGHT

Absolutely Nothing to Get Alarmed About

The Wig

The Messenger

Charles Wright

Absolutely Nothing
to Get Alarmed About

FARRAR, STRAUS AND GIROUX

NEW YORK

WITHDRAWN
UTSA LIBRARIES

Copyright © 1967, 1968, 1969, 1970, 1971, 1972, 1973
by Charles Wright
All rights reserved
First printing, 1973
Library of Congress catalog card number: 72-86414
ISBN 0-374-10036-5
Published simultaneously in Canada by
Doubleday Canada Ltd., Toronto
Printed in the United States of America

Much of this book first appeared
in *The Village Voice*

LIBRARY
University of
At San Antonio

*In memory of Langston Hughes,
Conrad Knickerbocker, and Alfred Chester*

I had never before understood what
"despair" meant, and I am not sure
that I understand now, but I
understood that year.
—Joan Didion

Life is worthwhile, for it is full of dreams and
peace, gentleness and ecstasy, and faith that burns
like a clear white flame on a grim dark altar.
—Nathanael West

Absolutely Nothing
to Get Alarmed About

IN THE HALF-WORLD of sleep where dreams and consciousness collide, I turned on the narrow, sticky plastic mattress. The brilliant ceiling light seemed to veer toward me. But with less than four hours' sleep, fourteen shots of vodka, six twelve-ounce bottles of beer, two speed pills, one marijuana cigarette —I chuckled in my pale, lemon-colored cubicle. The stone floor had a fresh coat of battleship-gray paint. After less than a week, the old terra-cotta paint was surfacing. The armless bentwood chair functioned as a night table. Narrower than a standard clothes hanger, the wardrobe was doorless. The new opaque window was jammed. Unlike other residents, I never came upon rats or snakes. What unnerved me were the goddamn arrogant cockroaches. Who cared? The cubicle was at least a roof, reasonably clean, reasonably safe and inexpensive, thanks to the charitable foresight of the Salvation Army's Bowery Memorial Hotel.

Now, the 6 A.M. voices of Sallie's men blended; became a litany of fear, frustration. Voices calling for ma, mama, and mother. Pleading: Stop and help—occasionally stamped with the moan of a dying male tiger. These nightmare voices were the twin of the daytime voices. These were weak men who no longer cared. Cheap wine chemicals had damaged their brains. As I listened, fear touched me. Would I become a soldier in their army? *Fool! Get yourself together. You've got to get out of here.*

Then my bowels roared. I bolted toward the bathroom. My timing was perfect. Afterward, pleased as a spoiled fat cat, I stood up and felt faint. Grabbed the door of the toilet booth. Too late, too late. I was falling, slowly, toward the tiled floor. Just another miniblackout.

My heart was racing. Perspiring, breathing hard, I eased up from the floor.

"You all right?" a voice asked.

"Yeah." I grinned sheepishly.

A tall man with a weathered face like Robert Penn Warren was staring at my naked body.

"I can see your ribs," he said. "You don't eat. Me neither. Here, have a swig."

I took a healthy swig from his bourbon pint, thanked him.

"You better watch it," he warned.

4

"That's the trouble." I chuckled. "I have been watching it."

Solitary watchman. Lantern held high. Peering out at friends, strangers. Desperately trying to get a reassuring bird's-eye view of America. F. Scott Fitzgerald's sunny philosophy had always appealed to me. I believed in the future of the country. At fourteen, I had written: "I am the future." Twenty-six years later—all I want to do is excrete the past and share with you a few Black Studies.

I felt as if my testicles were packed in a bowl of dry ice. Things beyond my control had rimmed my brain, and it was strange to relax in Brownsville where the death of a boy had forced boys of his own age to riot in his and their name, and I who had been contemplating suicide for five days no longer a boy.

Now in the wake of his death, sporadic action nipped through these fucked-up streets. A new R & B—rage and brutality. Sirens of police cars and sirens of unmarked cars. Smoke drifted from Howard Avenue like the smoke of an autumn bonfire. A tall old woman hobbled down from a stoop, cackling, "I knew it. They is started."

A car pulls over to the curb, and a man says, "I'll let

em pass, baby. They got their work cut out for them."

"You're right, brother," I replied. The P.R. bodegas were closing or closed. In fact, P.R.'s were in the act of disappearing, although they crowded their windows, talked, and looked down into the almost deserted arena of the street. No P.R. men were lounging against cars tonight. A few of them sat on stoops or braced themselves against Victorian carved doors.

I had to buy a six-pack in a bar and returned to the flat, popped a few, talked with Tony. TV gave out *Take Her, She's Mine*, while the sound of shots, Molotov cocktails, angry voices drifted across the vacant back lot (filled with about twenty-five inches of rubbish and where at this very moment a slender middle-aged Negro man was studying the lot as if it were a mound of old gravestones) and into the flat's windows.

There was absolutely nothing to get alarmed about. Just another domestic scene in current American life. But they will use more sophisticated methods next summer. The kids will have matured by next summer.

Earlier a group of them had stopped me.

"Have you seen Joe?"

"No, man," I said. "I ain't seen Joe."

A mistaken identity. But I was with them—someone has to be on their side and I cursed their goddamn parents and this goddamn mother-sinking country that has forced them into the act of rioting. In the act of reaching the portals of the seemingly prosperous poor, their parents had lost them just as this country had forgotten the parents.

Certainly I felt these black kids had a legitimate right to break store windows and throw rocks and bottles. Recently, I had worked at a resort where bored, wealthy kids kept the security guard on the go as they ripped lobby sofas and broke into the underground lobby shops between midnight and dawn.

Meanwhile, the black children will continue to riot and die.

M. D. said, "There is a man that I want you to meet." We taxied over to Intermediate School. No. 201, 2005 Madison Avenue, and I met the man. I also saw, for the first time in my life, former Senator Paul H. Douglas of Illinois, chairman of the L.B.J. Commission on Urban Problems, and Senator Robert F. Kennedy and two of his handsome children.

We arrived late, and I could not hear what Senator Kennedy was saying. It did not matter. He seemed likable. And despite the rumor of the ruthless reputation, the cold blue eyes, I could picture him having a pint with the boys at McSorleys Ale House. Discussing politics, history, books, broads. I began to warm up to him and was rather pleased to think: This is our next

President, '68 or '72. I might not have felt that way if I had listened to what he was actually saying.

Afterward, the crowd banked around Kennedy as if he were Jesus Christ or the son of Jesus Christ. I had never seen anything like it. Perhaps this was the op real-life version and I failed to realize it.

A few minutes later, the Senator's smiling daughter exited to a Cadillac. Father and son walked toward one of Detroit's modest models.

M. D. and I looked for a taxi. I heard an old black woman say, "Give me some meat. I don't want no bones."

You greedy meat eaters—this is where it is at.

We finished the typing session, rapped boredom out of the Vietnam war, raced minute cars, and had a wild game of cat and mouse around the dining-room table. Now it was almost midnight. An incredible moon outlined rooftops like a romantic proletarian stage set. But the voices of this tough territory were real and violent. Unflowery. Already that restlessness—peculiar to people with a remembrance of Mediterranean nights—had knifed me. Charlie Mingus was on the phonograph, and I went back into the dining room.

Clara Bow curls frame Anne's five-year-old face. "Sorry about that. You'd better buy some Beatles records," she said, her smile as refreshing as a slice of honeydew melon.

I began smoking filtered pot. There was a brief silence. Bruce, who is seven, jabbed me in the ribs. A charming clown of a little man, he neither smokes nor drinks. Surprisingly enough, the boys rarely curse and then mildly, like a tap on the shoulder.

Fire-engine-shirted Mick was drinking canned beer. He is nine years old. "We had to leave our father," he said, gesturing. His mannerisms, voice seem exaggerated. I believe these actions are nothing but excessive air from his vat of violence. "Man! He was stoned all the time and beat our mother."

Mick was interrupted by eight-year-old Ron. "That was in Jersey," he said, and then frowning, snatched the beer from his older brother.

Clasping her hands, Anne said, "I was born in Jersey."

"Shut your trap," Bruce said. "You don't know what you are talking about. You were born in New York. At Beth Israel."

"Charles," Mick said, "Ron and me was born in New Jersey, and the rest of them were born in Beth Israel. We moved after the apartment building caught on fire.

There was a deaf-and-dumb boy who was always doing things. One day he set the building on fire and we moved."

"Doing his thing." Bruce laughed, twisting on the bar stool.

"Bruce," Ron warned. "Cool it. He couldn't help it. No one loved him."

"God loved him," Anne said.

"Yes," Ron agreed. "God loves everyone. I've got a picture of him. Do you wanna see it?"

"It's Jesus, stupid," Mick said when Ron returned with a color reproduction and another can of beer.

"Mama's dancing," Ron said.

Then I heard heavy footsteps and lusty masculine voices in the hall, and we all looked at each other.

"I hope she doesn't get drunk," Ron said.

"Man! She's already stoned," Mick told him.

I wanted to hear Bob Dorough sing "Baltimore Oriole" and went into the living room. I heard Bruce whisper, "I'm going over and see what's happening. I'm gonna get some loot."

"Git some for me," Mick told him.

I could see their mother sitting at the chromed table, wearing the perennial purple-splashed muumuu gown. A pleasant, plump woman with a wardrobe of hair pieces, Nellie's teeth look like ancient Spanish gold. A dark-haired young man was behind her chair, tonguing her left ear, his long slender hands racing up and down her bosoms as if trying to determine their length and quality. Between "No, oh no!" Nellie moaned.

Mick eased over and peeped through the crack in the door. Anne was looking, too. Beatle-maned Ron did not get up. Pierced with cut-crystal sensitivity, he sat at the table writing his name over and over again.

"It's time for you to go to bed!" Mick exclaimed, slapping Anne violently. She screamed, her little arms outstretched as if to curtsy.

"Mick," I said. "Watch it."

"It's gittin' late, man."

"Do you wanna go to bed?"

"No. I ain't sleepy."

Now Anne was rolling on the floor, sobbing. Bruce soft-shoed back in. "I got it." He grinned. I helped him count $1.37 worth of silver.

"You have to pay for the party tomorrow," I said.

"What time?" he asked, unable to conceal his delight.

"Late in the afternoon. Root beer, potato chips, and ice cream."

Ron looked up and smiled for the first time. He reminds me of the Mexican-Indian children I saw on the road to Boca del Rio. He is going through a bad time. The girl he likes is no longer allowed to play with him, although she sends him notes by messenger. Ron is a fine looking, healthy eight-year-old. Quiet, well-mannered, he looks like the type of boy you'd want your child to play with.

Nellie called him. He returned with her glazed mug, singing "Georgy Girl," and followed me into the living room.

"Charles. Don't give her too much whiskey. She's drunk."

Ron took the Scotch to his mother, who was pushing a bereted, tall man out the door.

"No," Nellie said. "Get out. You hurt me. You're dirty."

Ron took the mug into their apartment and wouldn't look at his mother. Three-year-old Glen and the two-year-old twins, Mal and Bobbie, followed him to my place. Mal is always without his pants, and his brothers tease him. He shook his thumb of a penis at them. Ron wanted to get Mal a pair of pants. I told him to get some records from the bedroom. I did not want him to see his mother.

The tall dirty man had her nailed against the wall of the hall. Hula-grinding, she had her arms around him.

I closed the door, and Ron announced, "I want some more beer."

"You won't drink my beer," I said.

"I'll git it," Mick said. "Mama lets us drink beer, and it's Saturday night."

The two-year-old twins were boxing when Mick returned.

"Man!" he said. "She's got the lights off."

"Oh God," I silently moaned to the moon. But I knew there were seven children in the room. I would have to make something of the night, regardless of what had happened or would happen.

I lit another filter and announced, "All right. Let's see if you remember how to type your name. Everyone will type except Mick and Ron. They're drinking beer, and I don't want them to spill it on the typewriter."

"Oh man." Mick frowned. Ron took a long sip of beer, ran over, and put it down on the cabinet.

Nellie called me. I went to the door and walked across the hall. The lights were still off. Nellie was naked.

"Here's a present," she said, offering a newspaper-wrapped package, half the size of a bank book. "The kids no trouble?"

"No," I said. "And thanks."

"Mama's naked." Anne giggled.

"Shut up," Bruce screamed, and then all of the brothers ganged up on their sister on the blue-tiled floor.

I pulled them apart and plotted the typing lesson. All right. Knock it off. Anne is first. Everyone will have a chance to type. The twins will type too."

"Ah man," Mick said. "They're babies. They don't know nothing."

"Charles Wright," the young woman said, smiling. The young woman was a black reporter for a magazine. She was interviewing the writer for the magazine's forthcoming lead story, "The Real Black Experience." I had had a couple of pills and enough drinks to make me feel warm toward almost anyone I might run into between 5 P.M. and dawn. Certainly I felt very warm toward the lady reporter. We both had, in a limited sense, climbed the black progressive ladder in white America. It was a difficult time for blacks to be truly black in a black reality. It was very easy to get bedecked in an ethnic showcase. But I had been black for a very long time. Before black was beautiful. Marcelled blacks gave me the cold eye ten years ago. I had an uncoiffeured, bushy Afro. I loved blues, collard greens ("pot liquor," as the collard juice was called), ham hocks before they became fashionable. And now I faced the young black reporter with lukewarm charm. I knew the magazine's editor had supplied the questions. I was going to be a gentleman about the whole damned thing.

By the time we reached the Cedar Tavern, despair said, "Good-evening, old sport. It's me."

We ordered vodka martinis. The young woman had dinner. I had more drinks and was prepared for war, while she promised a truce in her Brooklyn Heights apartment. The young woman talked about her Italian holiday. Oh yes, Italian men. I ordered another round of drinks, forced charm. I was almost tempted to tell her about the postal cards of supermammary-blessed Ethiopian women, about Italy's invasion of Ethiopia. With the Pope's blessing, they went to war with dreams of boobs. The young woman had a most respectable pair of mammaries. But I no longer wanted them or her. We had another round of drinks and left the Cedar Tavern. At Thirteenth and University I said, "Wait a minute, cunt. I have to take a piss." I went inside the wide door opening of an antique shop and urinated.

The black female reporter started running toward Fourteenth Street and hailed a taxi. I watched the taxi move off. I laughed and said aloud, "Thank God."

I moved near Chinatown to get away from you. Then moved *beyond* Chinatown. The seemingly casual arrangement of fruits and vegetables in Chinese store windows intrigues me. Memory paints another Asian display: Mrs. Han's flower stall in Seoul, Korea. A small woman, Mrs. Han was aloof. She had two sons. One was rumored to be a very important Communist in North Korea. The other son, aged ten, lived with Mrs. Han. He was a very large boy for his age, but he did not help his mother with the white mums, rose-red peonies, dwarf lemon trees. He stayed in back of the flower stall and painted watercolors. American and allied soldiers were always pestering the boy. They wanted to take his picture, and they tried to bribe him. They wanted to take his picture and send it to the folks back home. The folks back home had never seen anything as funny as a star and cauliflower on a human face.

At 10 p.m. on August 7, the moon was full and the air had turned cool. Vincent Jew and Wing Ha Sze were returning from the movies, walking down Bayard Street, next to the Chinese Garden—a semi-official, peeling, red and white plaque says in English and Chinese, "Manhattan Bridge Park." José Ortez, his girl friend, and another young couple were on the same side of the street. They had been to a social club and were going toward the subway, they said later.

Returning from the liquor store with a chilled bottle of vino, I could not see them from where I was on the opposite side of the Garden, walking down Forsyth Street, about fifteen or twenty feet from the corner of Division. On the opposite corner, I saw a stocky young man standing next to the parking lot. He had shoulder-length dark hair, wore a light-colored shirt of the T-shirt style, dark trousers. A leather type of shoulder bag was strapped against his barrel chest. He fumbled with the bag and looked around as if uncertain which way to go. Then suddenly turned under the bridge, and out of my vision.

Normally, I'm spaced out, move with the speed of a panther. But that night I was relaxed, my stride slow. Emerging from under the bridge, I started up Bayard and heard the first popping sound. Leftover firecrackers, I told myself.

The street curves here and is not very bright. Remember: the moon did not glow like a white light. I heard voices, the sound of fast footsteps on the pavement, heard the popping sound again, saw near the curb two streaks of red-blue-yellow light, two thin slanted lines like the halves of two V's. It was a fascinating, blinding light. On the far side of it, dark figures ran.

The first person I saw was the stocky man, first in the middle of the street, then a few feet east of that light, running. I knew someone had been shot. I saw no one but him. Head held high, looking as if it were extremely difficult to breathe, he clutched that shoulder bag and ran, very fast for a man of his size. I did not know if he had a gun and decided to let him get a few feet in front of me before chasing him. He did not run in a straight line and headed down Market Street, which leads into East Broadway. He ran under the bridge and did not turn in the direction of Forsyth, where he had come from ten or fifteen minutes before. He continued east on Division Street. A car blocked me, and I lost him in the dark, then returned to Bayard Street.

Wing Ha Sze lay on the sidewalk in front of the entrance to the Garden. His head was on the curb. A small, slender man, he appeared to be middle-aged. Still breathing at the time, his blood streamed down Bayard and glistened in that half-bright light. Dazed young Vincent Jew clutched his right side and stood a few feet from Sze. Now and then Vincent looked around, his face in shock or pain. Then he'd look down at his friend. Vincent was wounded slightly.

Baldwin, a man of the streets, arrived. "Don't touch him," he advised Vincent, "until the police get here. They're down the street."

But Vincent Jew went over to his friend. The experienced Baldwin said, "Don't touch him. He's dead."

At the sound of fast footsteps, I turned and saw a policeman. He asked me to stand against the Garden wall and questioned Baldwin and Vincent. A squad car pulled up sharply, and a young policeman got out and grabbed me. "Hey! Wait a minute," I protested. The first policeman came to my rescue (if he had suspected me, I doubt if he would have left me unhandcuffed, unguarded, about ten feet from him in the semi-darkness). Already you could hear voices and knew people were approaching.

The first policeman asked me to get in the squad car.

I obeyed and sat on his copy of Sunday's *Daily News*. Other squad cars arrived. People began appearing as if God had snapped his fingers and created them by the Garden wall. All of them were peering in the car at me. I had that uncomfortable feeling which afflicts celebrated people: I was afraid the crowd would kill me. But I kept my cool, lit a cigarette, and looked out at them and saw José Ortez for the first time. Frequently the police park at Bayard and Chrystie Streets. They were there when they heard the shots. They saw Ortez running, they said, and added that although they fired six warning shots, Ortez did not stop. He was finally apprehended on Division Street.

A café-au-lait-colored man, his dark hair was kept in place with a thin, old striped tie, and he wore a fancy knit shirt, the type which is popular with blacks, Puerto Ricans, and Italians. His trousers appeared to be less costly than the shirt. He was handcuffed and had a serene, saintly expression.

Presently, Ortez, his girl friend, and her friends, Baldwin, and I were driven to the Elizabeth Street Station of the Fifth Precinct—a slum of a station. A disgrace to the city and the men who work there. All of us except Ortez were ushered into a large room. *Willard* graffiti were printed all over the room. *Willard* the rat horror movie.

Baldwin and I had a good rapport. Neither of us knew the other people. José's petite girl friend had an earthy sexuality, and she cried and cried and cried. The other young woman had the open face of a child. I might as well tell you: Charles Wright is a distrustful son of a bitch. But the girl friend, the young couple gave off the aura of good blue-collar people out on a Saturday night. If they were acting, their air of innocence was the world's greatest triangle act.

We were asked our names and addresses. Then they brought in Ortez and took him into a back room. The girl friend started crying again. Around 11 P.M. we went up to the fourth floor. "Willars hole," the wall read. That was the way it was spelled.

The five of us waited in the fingerprinting room for about twenty minutes before being escorted into another room—the large, depressing room of the detective squad. Bored, I began drinking vino. The detectives did not seem interested in my stocky young man or that he was white (later I would be asked if he were Chinese). I was asked to return to the fingerprinting room, where I drew a rough sketch of the stocky hippie, whom I believed to be an ordinary young man with the veneer of a hippie. Then I went over to the desk, read Vincent Jew's testimony on page 36 of a small tablet. He and Wing Ha Sze were coming from the movies, walking by the bridge (they were walking on the sidewalk. The Chinese Garden was between them and the bridge). A man came between them, then started shooting. Vincent Jew ran across the street, then ran back to his friend. Wing Ha Sze was D.O.A. A bronze-colored book of matches, advertising Joe's barber shop in Ridgewood, New York, was on the desk. That was all. Without being asked, I returned to the other room, finished my vino.

Policemen, detectives surrounded José Ortez like desperate bees around the sweetest of summer flowers. The girl friend was crying again. The other young woman picked blackheads from her husband's face. His close-cropped head was in her lap, and his eyes were closed. All of us were out of cigarettes, and I went out to get some.

On the first floor, I saw Vincent Jew and showed him my rough hippie sketch. Vincent did not remember seeing him or me. Puzzled, I left the station.

It was a quarter of two Sunday morning when I returned with the cigarettes. Policemen, detectives were in a jubilant mood like a group of men after the victory of their team. Ortez gave me a long grateful stare. I was angry that the police had forgotten about the hippie. He was certainly a star witness. The alleged weapon had no fingerprints on it. The killer had supposedly had the foresight to wrap a handkerchief around it before firing, afterward it had been tossed on the sidewalk. It did not matter now. They had their man. Why should I get excited? It was only an ordinary Saturday night murder.

A week later, things changed. The police were not so sure about their man. My irrelevant statement was suddenly valuable. Now, there were frantic phone calls. Visits by detectives, a visit to the D.A.'s office. I await a lie-detector test. All I can think of is a couple of lines from Jorge Luis Borges: "The acts of madmen," said Farach, "exceed the previsions of the sane."

"These were no madmen," Abulcasim had to explain. "They were representing a story, a merchant told me."

By the time you read this, the celebrating will have cooled. The friendly neighborhood grocer will be paid, the common-law husband will have met his pusher, and the children will be stuffed with sweets. Perhaps there will be a visit to Busch's, the famed credit jewelers, or a sharp new leather coat. The old-age pensioners and the "mentally disturbed and misfits" will pay their bar tabs and get jackrolled. However, all welfare stories are not grim. There are the old, the lame, and the helpless poor. This is their only way of life. But for others it is a new lease on living, almost as easy as breathing. Now all that remains are the twelve days of survival, the next check. I want to tell you about some of these men and women.

Mary X. is "off." Temporarily off. Brave, long-haired girl in midi-dress, the smart suède shoulder bag, living here and there. Starving. Almost tempted to take a job in a boutique. And why should Mary X. suffer in the richest country in the world? She had to miss Dionne Warwick at the Apollo and Soul Sister Franklin at Lincoln Center. She had been receiving her check at a friend's pad. But the caseworker paid a routine visit. "Where's Mary?" The friend's old lady said, "She ain't been here in over a month."

"And I'm off," Mary, who is twenty-nine, lamented. "Lying bitch. She's mad because I won't ball with them any more."

A few days later, Mary saw her social worker. Life is getting brighter. "Even if I have to go over there and throw a fit. Look, I haven't worked in four years. I could if I wanted to. But I think I need glasses, and I have to get my teeth fixed. And you know I have to take pills. I'm a nervous wreck." Speaking of a semi-drag queen who is almost at the top of the welfare-dollar ladder, Mary said, "That bitch. She gets $99.50 twice a month. And she's living in the street. I saw her trying to hustle over on the Apeside."

The Apeside is the East Village beyond Tompkins Square Park. In TSP I met Jojo. He was very uptight, his paranoia gave off sparks. "Man. They sent my check back. Got a cigarette?" Jojo, ex-garage mechanic. Blond, extremely bright, but frightened of touching his brain. He's spent three years in jail (robbery), dabbled in dope, and is now deep into a wine scene. He breathes like a man in deep pain. We stop off for a pint of Orange Rock. "Gotta steady my nerves, old sport." He smiles. We kill the pint, walk across town to the welfare haven on West Thirteenth Street, where the atmosphere is heady, hopeful like a theater where chorus gypsies are auditioning. I was surprised at the well-dressed welfare recipients. Radios, cassettes, everything was of the moment. A great many of them knew each other. Talked naturally of checks and who was off or trying to get back on. There were very few old people. *Mucho* preschool and school-age children, chasing each other between plastic, armless chairs. Like busy mothers everywhere, these paid very little attention to the children. They had plenty of time to gossip. Time to make love. And the well-lit, clean welfare haven was a pleasant place to kill time, wait for money, though a tense line shot through the undercurrent like a peak hour at the stock exchange. There might be some fucking hang-up, a cold cross-examination. Jojo sensed this. But we kept up a fast joking conversation, sliced with a few silences.

Almost three hours later, Jojo received a check for exactly $33. He would get more. He was properly modest. A serious Jojo faced the social worker. Welfare would arrange for a kitchenette pad. Jojo knew the ropes. After cashing the check, Jojo paid off a $7 loan, then invited me for beers, hard-boiled eggs. Later we switched to wine and watched the sports shoot pool. Life can be good for survivors.

Nellie will ball. Please accept my word: Helena will ball. "All I want to do is stay stoned every night," she once told me in lieu of an apology. There are few stoneless nights. Welfare money, booze, and beer from a platoon of male friends, sitting around the kitchen table, waiting on the free lay. Nellie has seven illegitimate children. Often they are hungry, thanks to their mother's careless life-style. Life in their mother's apartment has made them ferocious little warriors. Proud, the seven children are always on the defensive. It is only when they begin to trust you that they open up, play childish tricks, laugh. It is only then that, underneath it all, you feel as if melancholia is smothering them. I gave them candy, nickels, and dimes. I am tough, loving with them, and hope they understand.

But sometimes they avert their eyes. Melancholia becomes a dagger. They are disappointed: I will not marry their mother and become their father. It is only because of the children that I have never bedded the mother. Although my childhood was quietly religious and happy, I, too, was briefly a child of welfare. After my grandfather died, and before my father's World War II allotment, there was nothing my grandmother could do but apply for public assistance for me. It was a pittance in every sense of the word. Sometimes she did daywork for white families (in the village of New Franklin, Missouri, not too many white families could afford part-time help, much less full-time servants).

I remember that in winter we became the local F.B.I. of the railroad tracks, looking for coal that had fallen from the open-bellied freight cars. Even today I can taste the delight of a Sunday supper: day-old bread in a bowl of milk sprinkled with cinnamon and sugar. I remember the Christmas we were too poor to buy a tree. But luck was with us, one cold, sunny afternoon a few days before Christmas. We found clumps of pine branches along the railroad tracks. My imaginative grandmother decided that we would make a tree. We found a small leafless young tree and tied the branches to it. It was a beautiful Christmas tree, the delight of the neighbors. And we did not even have multicolored lights for the tree. I frame this memory briefly to let you know that I understand the plight of welfare. I hold no bitterness against those days. It was a happening of that particular time.

Yet there is dark music in the towns, cities, about the welfare recipients. We have to pay taxes to take care of these lazy, good-for-nothing bums. Still, there are the happy Lawrence Welk voices who sing, and this works to our advantage in the end. This is where we want to keep them. We will give them enough so they'll be content and will cause us no trouble. Welfare is their addiction.

Anyway, for those of you who are interested in trying yet another new life-style, here are a few surefire suggestions I have compiled with the help of Green Eyes, who never had to use them:

1. Become an addict.
2. Become an alcoholic or fake it.
3. Get busted, a minor bust, though you could have a fairly cool winter in the Tombs.

4. Get hepatitis.
5. Have a real or fake nervous breakdown. Take the cure at Kings County or Central Islip.
6. It is extremely possible for females to get liberated from work and money worries by getting pregnant.

Warning: Above all, remember to stay on good working terms with doctors. Get a written statement from them.

Now you're on your own, ducks.

THE AFTERNOONS OFFER MORE than a sharecropper's bag of humidity and rain. But the lunar boys are exceptionally cool, as if the age of Aquarius had instilled in them a terrifying knowledge of silence. In groups of twos, threes, and fours, wearing brilliant-colored nylon T-shirts, jeans, John's Bargain Store khaki walking shorts, tennis shoes, and athletic socks with deep cuffs, they are not long-haired. Immaculate, one of them wants to become a trumpet player. Another, at the age of fourteen, has had faggot grooming. Five of them are school dropouts. The boy with the "hot" $35 knitted shirts is one of six illegitimate children, all of them under the age of sixteen and on welfare.

These budding lunar professionals will, say between two and three of an afternoon, stroll into the Old Dover Tavern (the very "in" Bowery bar). In the beginning, at the end of the school term, they stood outside, while the leader entered. Later, as confidence ripened, they entered and huddled near the door, near the cigarette and candy machines. Now they prowl up and down the bar like altar boys, seeking some rare chalice.

The leader of one gang will ask the bartender for change or order his usual grilled-cheese sandwich. They never buy cigarettes, and it was only last Saturday night that we discovered that they have been trying to jam the candy machine.

Then silent, their young eyes revolving, they walk out into the wet, narrow plain of the Bowery (affluent infant of artist studios, rock-and-roll craters, German police dogs, Doberman pinschers).

Sometimes, the budding professionals will stop and rap with the wine-drinking afternoon bums. But these are really rehearsals, you might say. Scouting trips for boys with faces like stockbroking thieves. Boys who wait quietly for the oncoming darkness.

It's dark now, and they've made it over from the side streets. From the tenements and the public-housing projects in their clean clothes, as if it were the first day of school. I remember that the famed gang of late May and early June marched like stoned killers past the gloomy bank at Spring and the Bowery (the bank that is now a famous artist complex). This gang has been replaced by a gang that shoots in from West Houston.

And these clean-cut boys, ladies and gentlemen, jackroll the wine-drinking citizens of the Bowery. The take is small or nothing. Still, there are legends of the fabulous scores, the fine old gold pocket watch, false teeth, a social-security card, and sweet, dirty old dollar bills. But these boys have watched their older brothers jackroll, have watched the real pros jackroll, and have the act down solid, and it's all so cool, so clean. A cold, passive sport.

As one winehead told me: "They said, 'Pops. Got any juice?' I said, 'Howdy boys.' I was just setting there, on the ground. Too drunk to stand up and take a piss, and they came at me without another word. Just went through my pockets and took all that was left of the $34 I got for selling blood, plus the bonus."

Violent vistas are part of their heritage. But they are seldom violent with the wineheads. It's all so painless, easy. You do not even sweat. Occasionally, a winehead will get kicked in the teeth if he tries to fight back or calls the gang a bad ethnic name. Occasionally, a knife rips a coat pocket and there's a little blood. Occasionally, an old man is doused with gasoline and set on fire. But this is another breed of urban and suburban teenager. Affluent teenagers or stoned kooks.

No, these lunar lads are nonviolent in our luxurious age of violence. But they do not make the Bowery scene on the fifteenth and first of the month. This is big time and usually a black time. Real professional jackrollers. Black migrant workers, mainlined with the cheating stop-and-go sign of urban American and Catskill life. Damaged brains pickled in wine or cool small-time Harlem thieves down for the bi-monthly take.

On August 1, at seven in the evening, five blacks ganged up on one old white man at the corner of Prince and the Bowery.

Traffic jammed to a halt. The Bowery bar philosophers watched the happening. The white majority (Irish and Polish) were incensed by the bold black act. But they made no effort to do anything about it, except to spray two black regulars, two queens, with a water pistol of words. "Have I ever tried to rob you?" a hard-drinking black queen asked. "Shit. I could buy and sell all of you. Don't talk about my people."

Sitting four stools away, I suddenly laughed at the perverse reality of *this* sporting Bowery game.

The jackrolling blacks took from the old whites in the light of the day. At night the young whites drank freely of the old black queens and often stole from them, providing the queen bedded them.

Governor Rockefeller, campaigning for reelection, said yesterday that the addiction problem in the state had grown much bigger than he had expected four years ago.

The New York Times, August 4

"Young people today are being subjected to the most profound temptations and stresses—"

Robert Sargent Shriver,
The New York Times, August 6

"We didn't actually break in. The door was open so we just made ourselves at home."

"Hell. Charlie don't give a shit."

Sitting in the living room of a building marked for demolition, I wondered if I did care. After all, squatting out has become most fashionable. Earlier, I had been sitting in a bar, when an acquaintance had invited me to a party. In the past, I had offered Duk Up Soon a place to flop for the night, an occasional quarter, advice. This invitation was a thank-you gesture. And now we were in this living room, sitting on milk crates, a car seat, and the floor. Street lamps spotlighted the room. Votive candles created a ritualistic mood. The buffet: wine, pot, beer, and pills, plus the works. The kids were very polite, and I decided to sit in and see what would happen. Then Pepe came in. We were a little surprised to see each other; our smiles bordered on warmth. I had written about Pepe before, the summer jackrolling debut. Then Pepe's thing was pot, wine, beer, and glue. He was fourteen at the time. Now, almost seventeen, with a delicate dark mustache, sporting as always Italian knit shirts. Sneakers have replaced the $30 shoes. Sneakers are better for stealing, running. His welfare mother is now a redhead and still keeping the weekend lover. The other five children are in school and doing well. Pepe looks like a sharp vocational student as he takes the bags from the deep cuffs of his socks. Beaver has the works which until an hour ago were in a frigidaire on Avenue A. Leon, who weighs about 120 pounds, bends a Coke can and looks a little frightened as he takes off his belt and turns on. Duk Up Soon and Beaver, who had been jiving like pill-high jockeys, silently watch Leon. Envy seems to touch their faces like rain. But they have their turn at the needle and begin rapping. Beaver, tall and very lean, is tensely cool. He shoots, then jumps into the middle of the floor, the needle still in his arm. "Man. Look. Look at that! Man. A fucking bull's eye. I hit it every time."

Presently, Pepe began to nod. Leon played with the expandable key chain attached to Duk Up Soon's trousers. There were eleven keys on the chain. Only one fit Duk's transient door. Beaver, cupping his hand over his nose and snorting, began his clean-up campaign. "Man. This pad looks like a pig pen. I gotta have a clean pad. You should see my sisters' pad, a fucking dump." Watching him, I was listening to Frankie Crocker on WMCA. About an hour later, two teen-age boys and a very pretty girl walked in, peering into the semidark room, a little uneasily. They brought knockwurst, beans, and bread.

"Shit," one of them said. "You said you had a pad, and man you ain't even got a pan."

"Fuck," the pretty girl said to no one in particular. She is fifteen and has a voice like a Bingo Bronx housewife. But her voice grew louder, and she began to put down her two friends.

"Fuck off, Tommie. You creep," the pretty girl said, just before she turned on.

The two friends had turned on and wanted to leave. "Bitch. I'm gonna git rid of you," Tommie said. "Git your fucking ass together."

But the pretty girl was high now, going through the dumb-blond bit. She sat down on a milk crate, crossed her fine, bare legs, opened her fringed suède handbag, and began making up her face. It took her almost twenty minutes to paint her lips. "Dumb bitch," the boy friend taunted. The girl tried to put on false eyelashes with one hand and hold the mirror with the other.

"You ain't got no brains at all," the boy friend said, snatching the mirror from the girl's hand. The girl was very quiet now as if she were alone. Our voices with the rock music were the sounds of people who were in hell and would never get out.

"Well," I said finally, "I've got to make it."

They were damn nice kids, despite the junk. The rapping had mainly been for my benefit. It was their way of showing that they were with it. Why didn't I call the cops or the narc people? Well, I had talked to these kids and kids like them for a very long time. I knew they had to do their own thing. That is unless they were busted.

Just the other night, I had an encounter with the cops. "Why don't you do something about the junkies and pushers?" I said.

"You should go back to Spanish Harlem," the cop told me.

"Sorry. I'm not Puerto Rican."

"Then go back up to Eighth Avenue and 125th Street."

I laughed.

Junkies like scavengers overturn litter baskets, looking for the heroin that has been stashed there, or they circle the full green-leafed trees looking for the bags, and no one cares as a slim junkie (using a master key) opens a car trunk, directly in front of Daytop Village on Chrystie Street, and makes off with a flashlight, a battery recharger in the Chinese Garden (officially named Manhattan Bridge Park in English and Chinese). The young Chinese boys play a new sport: baseball. The sun is high in the watery blue sky, and it is a quarter of two in the afternoon. Three junkies shoot up, while on the bridge a hard-hat construction worker looks on in amazement: Yes S. X. was gagging to death, and the others were high and giggled, but Beaver comes in, drags S. X. to the bathroom for a cold shower and ice cubes on his testicles. Dial 911 and watch two teen-age boys steal a tire off a car at high noon. Later, I take a junkies count: two hours netted eighty-seven in a limited area, and I wasn't trying very hard. On Bleecker, a bearded hippie stops me with "Hey, baby. I need seven bags." Sorry, I say, and another cat comes up and asks what does that honky want, and I tell him, and the two of them make it to the corner, and one twothreefourfive sixseveneightnineten they are busted by a hip-looking detective on St. Mark's. The kids are always stopping me: I am amused because I look so junk hip, and in the Chinese Garden I watch—are you ready—two young men walk over to a tree where two junkies had turned on twenty minutes before; the two young men have a camera, and the fat boy takes off his belt, kneels down, pretends to shoot up as his friend photographs him. Who knows, fake shooting could become a fad in the careless season of real shooting.

And here I sit popping pills, drinking wine, weighed down with twelve pounds of grief for you, Langston, remembering the reply to your hospital note that I forgot to mail.

Por favor . . . forgive the delay. I think of you often.

Now try to rest and think of what you are working on and your future work. That is all except a little good loving . . . now and then.

Flores, flores . . . from the heart.

And then . . . When? I can't remember. During some full-fledged moment of despair, I had written on that note: Just let me close my eyes and die.

I am dying and you are dead. The people are in mourning. The press has given you the full-dress treatment. They are caroling about your charm, vitality, your prodigious output. Your humor. You were a very logical man who would have been a better poet and writer if you had not been born black in America.

Ah! *The Weary Blues* . . . your first book, which you discussed with me last month, sitting in the Cedar Tavern, drinking black coffee and brandy. I had a vodka with beer chaser and listened to your advice. You were one of the few real people I had met during the last two years. I remember you saying: "*The Wig* disturbed me, and it's a pity you can't write another one like it. But don't. Write another little book like *The Messenger*. When I was starting out. Man . . ."

A good night. That last cold night.

Ah! *The Weary Blues* . . . no mothergrabber, he did

not sell out to whitey with his simple tales. He did not even sell out to himself. He was born in another world. He created something that was real. One dares not mention that this was the only way for him to get published and that he had to eat and buy shoes. And none of it was easy. And it seems to me, Langston, that you knew what your literary black sons haven't learned: it's a closed game played on a one-way street.

Ah! The bitterness, some jiveass mothergrabber will say.

But we know better, don't we? The smile on your face in the white quilted coffin says so. The undertaker had a touch of genius, for the smile is nothing like your smile but the smile that was always underneath the surface smile. The smile that was in your voice and your laughter.

The serene mad smile of one who is trapped!

At the funeral home I heard a woman say, "Don't look like he suffered one bit."

No, no, no!

If you had lived, you would have been in Morocco now with the photographs and introductions I had given you. Florence, whom you met here, and Cadeau, the white Peke, were waiting for you. You spent four days in Tangier last year and liked it well enough to return and spend the summer there. That is, if you solved the money problem. And most of all you wanted to go to the folk festival in Marrakesh.

And it was strange that Tuesday morning, Langston. I hit the streets, slightly stoned, talk-singing that old Billie Holiday tune, "Good Morning, Heartaches . . . Here we go again . . ."

And there you were on the front page of *The New York Times*, dead.

I hated to leave you up on St. Nicholas Avenue . . . just when I had gotten to know you.

I hate to close this note, but I must put you out of my mind for the time being. And it is not your death that I'm mourning. It's the horror of it all. "Ah, Man!" you would chuckle sadly.

Poor black poet who died proper and smiling.

Langston Hughes was always concerned about my eating habits. Frequently, he invited me to dinner, restaurants or to his Harlem brownstone. I was always a smiling liar: "I have eaten, old sport. All I want is a double vodka on the rocks." But a few nights after his funeral, I returned to Harlem, buoyed with the memory of my black brother, the poet, who died proper and smiling. This buoyancy sunk as I walked through the streets of Harlem. It was like walking through the streets of Seoul, Korea, after the truce. Here the racial truce was a constant thing, almost as normal as the ultramarine evening sky, the tenements, the laughing voice of a woman describing the size of a rat ("a big cat without legs"), the expensive new cars, surreal against the backdrop of old decayed buildings. There were no stars, no breeze. The air was as potent as exhaust fumes. I walked around a long time that night, and the more I walked, pain and hunger increased like the folds of a fan. I went into a small clean "down home" café, ordered a double helping of barbecued spareribs, collard greens, potato salad, cornbread. I even ate two slices of sweet-potato pie. Good vibrations engulfed the café. The motherly owner, circles of thick braids wreathing her head, a bib apron fronting a sagging bosom, ample stomach, called me Sonny. I felt very much at home, savored the warmth, brought it back downtown like a doggie bag, then lost it.

A perfumed note from Paris.

Dear Charles:

I am staying in Anne T.'s flat on the Ile St. Louis. The poor thing had to go to Portugal for a holiday. So I'm alone and damned glad. Most of the Parisians are holidaying too, and I avoid the American tourists. Avoid quaint bistros where I'll be cheated anyway. I go out only to walk Bebe. Anne's Spanish maid is a jewel. My Costa del Sol Spanish comes in handy. I'm doing a little needlepoint, and yesterday I made a chocolate mousse. Hon, I'm simply laying low, working crossword puzzles, reading detective stories. I've even read *The Little Prince* again. I've gained a little weight and am almost my old self again. And you *know* what happened to me in the States. My goddamn family. A bunch of fucking rats! But don't be surprised if I should suddenly turn up, unannounced.

Take care. Bebe sends his love.

Maggie

P.S. I FORGIVE YOU!

"Oh Jesus," I moaned, letting the wheat-colored note fall to the floor. "I forgive you," Maggie had written in caps. Maggie, it is a new season. I got up and discovered that I was out of Nembutals. Despite the succulent soul dinner, I did not have enough energy to masturbate. So I polished off a quart of Orange Rock wine, about a third of Chambray vermouth, chain-smoked, and tried not to think.

Around midnight, I hit the streets. No heralding trumpets greeted me. No royal streets led to the House of Orange. However, Hershey's Bowery bar became an orangerie, a smoky crimson stage where approximately thirty-five intoxicated men tried to upstage each other. Like ash-can whores, they tried to con each other and the bartender. A mangy, crippled dog sauntered in and bequeathed fleas. I ordered another wine, looked up at the mute television, which seemed to gradually rise toward the ceiling. Unlike the drinking men, the television apparently wanted to get closer to God.

That's when I turned, looked out the door, and saw the girl. I ran to the door and watched a black teen-age girl walk down the Bowery. Walking as if it were day and the street, a pleasant, tree-lined country lane.

I caught up with the girl and remembered where I had first seen her, playing softball in Chrystie Street Park about a week before. She played very well and commanded every male's attention. What I'm sure most of us were admiring was not her pitcher's left arm but her ice-cream-cone tits, the wide womanly buttocks, although she appeared to be no older than sixteen.

"Hello," I said. "Where are you going?"

"Home," the girl replied, averting her eyes.

"You shouldn't be out this late alone."

"I was over at my girl friend's on Houston. We were listening to Smokey Robinson and the Miracles, and I forgot what time it was."

"Where do you live?"

"Ludlow," the girl said, sounding like an eight-year-old.

"Do you want me to walk you home?"

"If you want to."

In the beginning, I had told myself that I wanted to protect her like a brother, like a father. But when we reached Delancey Street I had my arm around her. She rested very easily in my embrace. Innocent and sweet fantasies waltzed through my mind. But the Midwestern, Methodist country boy did not applaud the waltz.

"I don't have to go home yet," the girl told me, looking straight ahead.

We crossed Delancey and walked through the park, deserted except for winos bedded on the pop-art-colored benches and a group of teenagers smoking marijuana. Their transistor gave out with the driving Jackson Five.

Once we stopped and kissed. The girl offered her lips willingly. There was desperation in her caress. I wanted to have her in bed, all night. I wanted to wake up with her in the morning. My hotel was out of the question. But at the far end of the park, beyond the recreational building, the land sloped. Large old trees formed a canopy, blocked the light. The wide ditch was cool and dark, and we went there and made love. The early-morning hours were delicious.

Now I was managing to write for *The Village Voice* every other week, supplementing that income with an occasional slop-jar job; washing dishes in penal delis, carrying one-hundred-pound bags of rice on my 129-pound shoulders. But I had my big toe in the door of my world again. The dusty black telephone which sat on the floor like a discarded toy and never rang except when management called bitching about the rent began ringing. There were letters, invitations to parties. I began seeing old friends again. One of the best was beautiful black Hilary, an artist-model.

After a pushcart hot-dog lunch, we decided to go into the Cedar Tavern and have a few drinks.

On the fourth Scotch and water, Hilary said, "You must be more social, Charles. Parties are where things happen."

"And don't happen. I'm tired of assholes and freaks and phonies."

"Now, baby," Hilary pleaded.

"Shit, Hilary," I exclaimed. "I wasted a whole weekend with those black middle-class cocksuckers on Long Island. Why? Because I was promised a job. And all they wanted to talk about was my experiences in Tangier and Mexico. Plus the hostess had 'always wanted to write.' Shit. Let's have another drink."

Hilary giggled. "At this rate, I'll be stoned before I get to the Art Students League."

"Won't be the first time, babe," I said, signaling to the waiter.

Hilary reached over and played the piano on my left hand. We got along damned well.

"Grit your teeth and curl your toenails," Hilary said absently.

"That's right, cupcake."

"T. C. Moses is having a party Friday night. And he asked me to see if I could get you to come."

"Is he still screwing that fat blonde?"

The waiter arrived with the drinks. Hilary's timing was perfect: "Do you think that nigger is gonna give up all that vanilla ice cream?"

"He might as well get it here. He sure as hell can't get it in Greensboro, North Carolina."

Joshing, Hilary cleared her throat and said grandly, "Baby, I'm waiting on your answer."

"I don't know." I sighed. "You know the last good party was the one that Bob Molock gave for me. That was nice. I like Bob. He's got balls."

"Are you coming?" Hilary wanted to know.

The night of T. C. Moses III's party was extremely warm. I had spent the day delivering circulars from door to door in Yonkers. Even an extremely fast Doberman pinscher could not catch fast Charlie. The weather, frustrations, the small circular check could not bring me down. I was laid back. With my cool. I even listened to a right-wing, country-western station. Relaxed, once I had bathed. I popped a couple of bennies, siphoned off the last of the vodka. It was almost 10 P.M. now, and I put on my party costume, which was nothing but a pair of clean blue jeans, a button-down drip-dry white shirt, a pair of second-hand imitation Gucci black shoes that I had bought on the Bowery for three dollars.

Once upon a time, Manhattan's upper West Side was a slum except for the splendor of Central Park West, West End Avenue, and Riverside Drive. The police and underground knew it as the playground of drug addicts and flaming drag queens. But that seems a long time ago. A decade? Today it is known chiefly for Lincoln Center, expensive remodeled brownstones, and as the province of the literary and artistic Jewish Mafia. Yet another breed has staked out part of the West Side for its own. A strange black breed that was conceived in the idealistic Kennedy years, passed their youth in Johnson's Great Society, grew to maturity, prospered in the subtle South Africa of the United States of 1971. The majority of these young black men and women are clever, extremely intelligent. The majority of these young black men and women are only superficially militant. Of course, they give money to black causes and buy the Black Panther newspaper (how can they refuse with their manner and dress on a blue-sky Saturday afternoon?). All of them agree that New York's finest pigs are "terrible. Just terrible." And like skimming fat from milk, they are as bourgeois as a Republican Vice President. Y'all hear me? Riot all over the goddamn city, but don't bomb Macy's, Gimbels, or Bloomingdale's. Do not open a drug-addict center within five hundred miles of Tanglewood.

Some of these young black men and women are my acquaintances. I knew and liked T. C. Moses III. I was finger-popping as I rang his doorbell.

T.C., who went to Howard University, received his law degree from Columbia University, sported a conservative Afro. Dark-skinned, he wore an English suit, white shirt, and dark tie. Smiling warmly, he shifted one of his sixteen pipes from his right to his left hand.

"Charlie. My main man. We've been expecting you."

"Sorry I'm late." I smiled, hoping it was real.

Just then, Julie, the fat blonde in something long, flowing, and purple, squealed. "Angel, baby," she cried and gave me a solid hug, about a dozen wet, little kisses. She smelled of gin and perfume.

We went into the white-walled living room with its highly polished floor, garden of green plants, paintings, and drawings by black artists. As far as the eye could see, fake imported African artifacts took possession of walls, floor, tables. The most imposing had their own lucite pedestals (T.C. went to Africa last year and forced a protesting Julie to remain in Paris).

The lights were low, people milled about like museumgoers. Aretha Franklin was on the stereo, and I knew it was party time. Time for most of them to let their hair down about an inch. Earlier the music would have been a little Bach or a Mozart fanfare, and the talk would have been heavy: the fate of mankind, crime in the street, and that man in the White House and how are you, my dear, and Sybil is in the country for the weekend. "What you drinking, sport?" T.C. asked.

"Double vodka on the rocks."

"Got it."

"Look who is running, running." Julie giggled.

Who else could it possibly be, dressed in silver from head to foot. Hilary. She grabbed me, and we went off to a corner.

"Cupcake. Take it easy."

"Give me a kiss," Hilary said in a pouting little girl's voice. "Party's a drag. Let's go somewhere and fuck."

"Be sweet," I warned.

"Be tweet," T.C. repeated. "Hilary, I want Charles to meet Mr. and Mrs. Roosevelt Robinson."

"All right," Hilary was suddenly serious. "I'll be goody-good if you get me another Scotch, love."

And off we went to meet Mr. and Mrs. Roosevelt Robinson. Mr. and Mrs. Robinson were in their early thirties and stood against the curtainless picture window that overlooked the Hudson River. They were an attractive couple and seemed slightly uncomfortable. But we managed to make smooth small talk. I found them pleasant. They had heard of me and were properly thrilled. Neither of them had read my two books.

"Darling," Hilary cooed. "Charles is looking for a job, and I know you have connections with that urban youth thing . . ."

"I'll give Mr. Wright . . . Charles, my card." Mr. Robinson beamed, looking directly down into Hilary's Mount Rushmore bosom. Mrs. Robinson looked first at Hilary, then back at Mr. Robinson.

Hilary was wound up now. She squeezed my moist hand. "Charles is so talented. And we wouldn't want him to have to wash dishes forever, would we?"

I wanted to talk and comfort the attractive couple, Mr. and Mrs. Roosevelt Robinson. But all I could say was, "Hilary's stoned, and it was nice meeting you. Excuse us please." Escorting Hilary toward the bar, I teased, "Oh, you bitch. You screwed that deal."

"Fuck'm. Fuck'm. Phony shitheads."

"If I don't get a drink," I chuckled, "this new mass department-store culture will smother me."

Before we could reach the bar, a black voice commanded, "Charles Wright!"

"Oh Charles," Hilary said. "It's A.X. and his gentleman friend, the poet." A.X.'s court consisted of two white men and one serious, plain young woman who looked as if she was a graduate of an expensive avantgarde girl's college and might at one time have considered joining the Peace Corps. A.X.'s poet was Afroed, bearded, serious, wore a rumpled suit and tie. He was searching. "Trying to get the feel, baby"—for a proper African name. Africa was where it was at. Poetry was where he was at.

"But is it art?" I wanted to know. "And why do the majority of black poets sound alike. I'm not talking about the kids from the street."

"But there's a war going on. We're at it with whitey," the poet said dramatically.

I looked at A.X. He nodded gravely. Was he thinking of his Irish doorman, who said, "Good evening, Mr. Coombs"?

"I wanna dance." Hilary pouted. "I wanna dance with my dress up over my head."

"Hilary," A.X. said, "there are ladies present. You are not in the Village."

"And, my dear, you are not in the subway john on your knees."

"Hilary," I exclaimed, pulling her away.

"Let's have a drink and drown all the schmuck faces. Am I really naughty?"

"Never," I said, bestowing a prize kiss on her unlined forehead.

A week later, a Monday, following the Newark riot, I was delivering circulars door to door in the Bronx. Now a good circular man is aware of dogs. Therefore, I stuck the supermarket throwaway in the iron gate, which was open. A healthy young dog came running from the side garden with his teeth bared. I managed to grab the gate; the dog, hunched like a quarterback, tried to chew my left foot through the fence.

"Don't kick him," a woman screamed. "This ain't Newark."

In the voice of a serene, opium-smoking saint, I replied, "I was not trying to kick your dog, madam. I was merely trying to close the gate. I didn't want him to bite my foot."

The fury had left the woman. "Oh, he won't bite you. He just don't like mailmen." My country 'tis of thee. Sweet land of old prejudices and new-old hates! A week before, a black co-worker and I had worked very hard to enjoy a long break. It was a very hot day and we were very thirsty. A neighborhood park was directly across the street. My man decided to go over and drink from the fountain. The scene didn't look kosher to me. Like some rare, two-legged bloodhound, I can scent a cracker neighborhood before you can snap your fingers.

There were teenagers in the park with that vibrant end-of-school-term air. I did not join my man at the drinking fountain. He returned, complaining, "They don't want you to even drink water. 'What is this neighborhood coming to?' one of them chicks said."

Naturally, I did not brood over what might happen to her neighborhood—a neighborhood where the majority of the people do not even read *The Reader's Digest*. Their mentality ran the gamut from the *Daily*

News to the *National Enquirer*. The small old houses are kept in good condition. The lawns, the size of twin bed sheets, are green and mown. There are birdbaths, statues of the Virgin Mary, pink plastic flamingos, reindeer, climbing roses, interspersed with plastic turquoise roses (the famed Burpee flower growers would not be pleased). Many of the mothers look hard and tired and have voices like seasoned soldiers. This is hardly my idea of a neighborhood that I'd want to move into. My man, born in Harlem, wants to die there.

I want to die under a Moroccan blue sky. I want to die where I can get a drink of water. I want to die in a country where rioting will produce emotions other than boredom. It seems, despite the looting, the wounded, the dead—an extremely mild happening. The fact is, I was rather disappointed. What would have been marvelous is that the ugly old city should have burned to the ground. This shock and a minor little civil war would perhaps force us to face the cold cunt of reality. Blacks would lose the war. But we have nothing to lose but our lives, and that doesn't seem very important in the present climate.

That rude bitch of sweet dreams, Mama Nightmare, has hung me like a polka dot, like a black Star of David,

55

below the fascist, Germanic clouds of South Africa, U.S.A.

She has been with me for a very long time, even before I could read and write. The guys at Smitty's gas station in Boonville, Missouri, called me dago. Aged five, I knew dago was not nigger. But they have remained stepbrothers to this day, forming an uncomfortable army with kike, Polack, poor white trash. But I had nigger, Negro, coon, black, colored, monkey, shit-colored bastard, yellow bastard. Perfect background music for nightmares. The uric sperm of those years has flooded my mind. Was I ever Charles Stevenson Wright? In private moments, I say aloud, my face igniting a sulphuric grin, "Your name is Charles Stevenson Wright." Occasionally, I applaud this honest sea dog facing me. Charles Stevenson Wright, the man. Face myself or else suffer the living horrors, the grind of a real fuck, guaranteed to keep you moaning until death.

Inherited bitterness, barriers, color nightmares. A rainbow then. Not Finian's "I've an elegant legacy waiting for ye," but a remembrance of you trying to rim the daylights out of me in the hope of producing another petrified black boy. My grandfather, Charles Hughes, was a boy at the age of seventy. It is remembering my grandfather and all the other boys who have been buggered through the years by that name.

Like a quarterly, ghostly visitor, one nightmare always returns. I am facing a Kafka judge (perhaps a god) and his court. Their skin and hair are as clear as rain water. The quiet is frightening.

"But I always thought I was simply Charles Stevenson Wright," I protest desperately, then roar with mad laughter, knowing that whitey, too, has great problems, nightmares. At this stage of gamy, Racial American Events, it is impossible for whitey to produce good niggers. But he still is capable of producing Uncle Toms. But always remember: hoarded prejudices beget slaves who impale their masters on the arrow of time.

DAY AND NIGHT, night and day. An end-
less freight train chugging through memory, braking
against the present. The enormous blast of the engine
is a proclamation of exhaustion, a depressive motif of
summer. Another summer on urban Hades. Pollution,
Violence, and Corruption are the gods here. The young
protest, riot. Their elders bite their lips, inhale anger,
or flaunt their power. Nailed between two worlds, I try
to stay stoned, clang like a bell in a small tower, comforted with the knowledge that I'm moving, moving on.
Get it! Get it! Get it!

I've moved again, moved near the financial district,
two blocks from City Hall. The streets are always
jammed. Jammed to the point of being stationary like
a motion-picture still. Then, as if a powerful switch had
clicked, the crowd becomes animated, moves on, goes
through the repertoire of living, boogalooing between
gray inertia and the red-hot scream of progress. They
are as dedicated as a perverse Communist. Silent or

vocal, the white and black American majority fills me with nausea and a suffocating sense of horror.

It is morning. My room is in the only hotel in the district. High ceilinged, half its former size, due to progress. The walls have a fresh coat of paint, Puerto-Rican-blue; small deep blue bottles highlight the paint. The large Victorian porcelain washbasin is a monument to another age of splendor. But the bentwood hatrack and chair, the vile painted furnishings dominate—a seedy stage for Tennessee Williams or Graham Greene (the stage is not waiting for me; I live here). But the mattress is clean, firm, and makes me feel good. Already I am debating whether I should christen it with the pretty black junkie girl. A daily visitor, Betty is always trying to "straighten up your pad, man," asking me to kiss her, or doing one of those brief junkie naps. I "respect" her; we get along damn well. But pride and the cold technician have always kept my emotion in check. At the end of each visit, Betty looks me straight in the eye and announces, "I will be back."

And Betty always leaves something. Things that females can't bear to part with in this age of liberation.

Bopping through a pauper period, I have nothing of value for Betty to steal. "Would you take money from me?" she asked.

"Nope," I replied.

"What about a little gift?"

Betty could steal a "boss" pair of sunglasses or an umbrella (it was raining that afternoon).

"Oh Charles." Betty pouted, then laughed madly, displaying a solid gold wristwatch she had taken from a man in a West Side motel.

Depression knights my forehead. I cannot move.

Finished the wine. The lukewarm beer, a bummer. I go to the window. The gray street looks fresh and clean after the rain. Directly across the street, the city branch of Swiss Farm nurseries displays young green trees, plants, and flowers in red clay pots. I am seized with hunger for the country, the sea. Surrounded by the Hudson and East Rivers, the Atlantic Ocean, I second Eugene O'Neill's cry: "I would have been much happier as a fish." Yet like an addicted entomologist, I am drawn to people. Let them flutter, bask, rest, feed on my tree. Then fly, fly. Fly away. Goddamnit. Fly motherfuckers.

In the afternoon, bless the solitude, salute it with vodka. Finished reading Henry Green's *Loving* and Muriel Spark's *Memento Mori*. Talk about a good high.

Read a paragraph from an Imamu Amiri Baraka essay (no matter, no matter. I remember LeRoi Jones when he lived on Third Avenue and was married to Hattie Jones. It was the beat generation then).

"We own despair," Imamu writes. "And then some cracker sits in space with a part in his skull and lectures about what we need. What we need. What we need first is for him to cut out."

Turning on the black radio for a little afternoon jazz, a white Southern woman tells a radio reporter in a voice like bitter, congealed honey: "Governor Wallace? He's a gone man."

Voices of a hall argument penetrated the door like the blade of a power saw.

"Do you want my woman?" A black male asked.

The white male reply was cautious. "Addie's a friend."

Stoned, Addie seconded the reply: "Dickie, I've lived here a long time. Since way back in 1968. Jefferson, Dickie's young. Younger than I am. He just got back from Vietnam, the poor thing."

"Yeah," Dickie shouted. "Vietnam! And I'll——any man that fucks around with my woman. Do you wanna fight?"

"Do you wanna fight?"

"Dickie . . ."

"I said, by God, do you wanna fight?"

"No. There's nothing to fight about."

A long silence until Addie said, "Why don't you two grown men stop it. I never seen such carrying on. They won't even let me have a dog for protection."

"I just don't want no white motherfucker . . ." Dickie began.

"Dickie," Addie pleaded. "I've lived around white people for forty-eight years. But that white son of bitch down at the desk won't let me have even one little old dog."

No, it was not a *Daily News* robbery, a typical lower-echelon robbery (estimate of "goodies": $800–$1,000), powdered with the frost that occasionally makes living in the City of Dogs interesting.

The facts: At 10 A.M. one morning, a budding thief climbed up the fire escape of a building on East Eleventh Street, then, with the skill of an acrobat, raised an unlocked window and climbed into a front fifth-floor apartment. The thief, a thirteen-year-old boy, was familiar with the apartment, having visited many times. A chubby Tom Sawyer type, he lived two floors below in a rear apartment. He had given one of the two occupants a perverse young female dog. The boy fed Blackie and unlocked the entrance door. But he exited by the fire escape, lugging a brand new tape recorder.

A cardiac man (a constant people watcher) saw the boy and called his wife. The couple lived directly across the street and watched our Tom try to hawk a "heavy, black case." Watched until the boy disappeared out of their view. Shortly after this, the boy returned, minus the tape recorder. The cardiac man did not have a phone, but vowed to tell the people in the fifth-floor apartment about the "heavy, black case." The Welfare Bonanza was nine days off, and it was a gritty time for the poor, especially for people who lived beyond the monetary welfare standard, for party people. But the couple across the street saw chubby Tom's mother dash out and return with "heavy goods" from the Pioneer supermarket.

Now it was almost 11 A.M. Eugene, one of the occupants of the apartment, returned and found the apartment in a shambles. He called his cousin Dash, who arrived an hour later. By this time, the police had arrived and departed. Dash waited for the detectives. Then it was time for Gene to go to work. Dash called me. I arrived at 3 P.M. and performed amateur spadework. The locked American armoire was almost unhinged. The two doors were like two flags at half mast.

"Well," I said, "I doubt if it was a junkie. They didn't take clothes or record albums. And the phones are still plugged in. They could have taken Gene's stereo. It isn't that heavy."

Laughing sadly, Dash, an IBM man said, "But they took the tropical fish and the bird."

Blackie, the perverse little bitch, had eaten the other bird. "I have a funny feeling," Dash said. "I bet it was the little boy downstairs."

Tom's boyish charm seemed too smooth, like rich country butter, and I had been watching him for a long time.

"I've been thinking the same thing."

It was now around five, and the sky was an explosion of red, and we eased the pain with Gordon's gin and waited for the detectives.

"Call the detectives again," I said.

"Hell. I've called them three times. They said they'd be over."

"Well, call them again. What have you got to lose?"

The man on the phone at the Fifth Precinct had a happy-go-lucky voice. He wanted to know if anything of value had been taken. I gave him a rundown. Yes, he said—that's a little money. Did he have a rough idea when the detectives would be over? No—but rest, rest assured, they would be over. Yes, sooner or later, the detectives would be over.

Around midnight, we had definite proof that Tom was our man. The window-watching man and his wife would testify. In court! By this time, we all were a little high and laughed and joked and waited for the detectives. Blackie defecated on the bathroom floor and ate it.

Gene and Dash worked on Saturday, and I stayed in the apartment with young Blackie. Each time I went to the refrigerator for a beer, the little bitch tried to grind against my leg. Jesus. What a dog. But: this is the City of Dogs. Mongrelsville. Sanitary-minded people let unleashed dogs roam at will and defecate on the sidewalk. These people probably wash their hands before leaving the bathroom. But they seem to suffer from the Camelot illusion that the city is their urban estate.

Our Tom is a collector of dogs. He charms people into giving him dogs or steals them. He houses the dogs in the wrecked basement of the Eleventh Street building. Sometimes he will find a man or a woman or a young hippie couple and croon with raffish charm: "Mama won't let me keep Rover. Will you take him home, and may I visit him sometimes? I love him, and he is a good dog."

Our Tom will visit Rover or Susie and take a buyer's astute inventory of your flat or studio. Already, he knows your work schedule as well as you. And I knew a great deal about chubby Tom. Knew that he was one of five children, that his mother had been forced to move from East Sixth Street, that she was husbandless, that it was always party time in their apartment. I also knew that the thirteen-year-old boy took dogs and threw them off the roof. These dogs usually belonged to neighbors. He was the talk of the block. The police arrived a few times, but nothing ever happened. Something was always happening to Tom's sister: she was fourteen and whored.

Dash arrived at 4 P.M. and called the Fifth Precinct. About an hour later, two policemen arrived, and the four of us stood in the bedroom and went over the robbery again. One of the policemen was silent. He was chubby and might have been Tom's father. The other policeman was young, slender. A philosopher. He said, rather sadly, "There isn't much proof to go on."

"If you don't catch the boy with the goods, what other proof could you possibly have? Except a man and woman who saw the boy—and our willingness to testify."

Up to this point, the slender policeman had ignored me. Now he gave me his attention. We talked about crime in the street, kids. I wanted to go to the bathroom. Finally, we said goodbye, and the two men in tired blue departed. Once again Dash and I got high and waited for the detectives.

Sunday was sunny and pleasant after the rain. It was also a busy day for our Tom. Apparently he sensed that something was up, for he was in and out of the building about ten times. But we never saw him.

Later that morning, the detective who had been assigned to the case called. He warned us not to talk to the boy or harm him. And please, please, do not stage a personal raid on his mother's apartment. The detective would be over later in the day with a search warrant. He was an overworked, sympathetic man, who arrived on East Eleventh Street at exactly 6 P.M. that Sunday evening, almost three days after the robbery had taken place.

It was party time in Tom's mother's rear apartment. A toast to the delight of Miller High Life. Music, laughter created a stereophonic noise in the crowded, dimly lit four rooms. The detective had trouble getting in; people pushed and ran from room to room, at times creating the effect of a crazy, jet-paced counterdrill. There was almost no furniture in the apartment. All the detective could do was issue a summons to Tom's mother. They were requested to appear in Juvenile Court.

Dash and Gene arrived at Juvenile Court. It was 9 A.M. Their case came up at 2 P.M. Tom's mother would not accept legal aid. She would get her own lawyer. The judge warned her not to return without a lawyer. A new date was set for the trial.

But the sullen woman returned without a lawyer. She was alone and occasionally smiled at the judge.

Where was our Tom?

In a clear, today-the-sun-is-shining voice, Tom's mother told the judge, "He didn't feel like coming."

The brief silence in the courtroom was deadly. The judge was outraged and issued a summons for Tom's arrest. He would be placed in Juvenile jail until the case came up again. Tom's mother made a quick exit from the courtroom. The sympathetic detective said, "I'll let you know when we pick up the boy."

That was almost five weeks ago. Sitting over a lazy Sunday-afternoon drink, I asked Dash about the case. But he changed the subject and talked about getting laid. We had another drink and listened to Richard Harris sing "Didn't We."

Then I remembered a UPI report: "Hove, England— The City Council has voted to build fourteen more public toilets for dogs, following experimental use of six fenced compounds equipped with dummy light posts."

Case dismissed. Dogs. Dog lovers.

ANOTHER CASE VIA AIRMAIL, another
perfumed note from Paris, France.

Dear Charles:

Anne T. returned from Portugal with a terrific sun-
tan and bruises. Bruises, hon. The poor thing is black
and blue, thanks to a fat, Princeton type of young man
(he said he was working for the C.I.A. "Top-level
stuff"). This young man stole a twenty-dollar bill off
Anne's dressing table. She left it there deliberately.
And now she's back, all bruised up, and wants to go to
the south of France. But I haven't got a bathing suit.
I haven't bought a thing all year except hose and a
panty girdle. I'm so poor. George's alimony is a pittance, and I was such a fool. I should have taken that
bastard to the cleaners. But I was thinking of the
kids. *His* kids. I never could conceive, and I'm too old
now, anyway. All I can do is play solitaire, work crossword puzzles, and read detective stories. Paris is terrible, terrible. The City of Lights doesn't mean a damn

thing to me any more. I'm seriously considering returning to the States. Ask Miss Feldman or Mr. Miller
at the Albert or those nice people at the Hotel Van
Rensselaer. I must live in the Village. Gone are the
Barclay days! Have you seen Charles Robb or that
bitch Hilary? I hope you are writing and everything is
going well. I'm baking bread and drinking black-
market Scotch. That's Paris for you. Bebe sends his
love. He still thinks he can talk. Silly dog.

Love,

Maggie

Maggie, I say aloud. Someone on the sixth floor threw
an empty beer can down into the courtyard. Maggie.
The former country-club wife. The little match girl. A
Chesterfield girl in World War II. It comes as a surprise to remember that she is white, that her eyes are
blue. What surfaces first is Maggie in a yellow dress
and dinner in a graveled court in Seville. Ma Griffe and
Joy perfume, a chemist's supply of pills, booze. Maggie
desperately trying to keep me from writing. Dear Dr.
Joyce Brothers, have you seen Kafka lately?

Remembering, feeling black, I have a stiff vodka,
hear heavy footsteps on the muddy brown floorboards
of the hall. Footsteps like an aggressive soldier, then
swift taps on my door, instantly telegraphing stoned

horrors. The hoarse voice calling, "Charles, Charles," sounding like a man who was resigned to silence and closed doors.

I opened the door. Clancy swung in, shadowboxing. "Man. Goddamn."

"Hello, sport."

"Look." Clancy beamed. "A whole fucking gallon of pure grape wine. Pretty, ain't it?"

"You got money? Baby, we'll have a snowstorm in August."

"There you go. I made a little score. Do you want me to go out and get you a sandwich, cigarettes?"

"No, Clancy."

"Well, let's drink the juice and screw the moose. Hey, I like that. Screw the moose."

"What happened to Martha?"

"Man. That bitch is crazy. She starting fucking with my mind. I can't stand anyone fucking with my mind."

An occasional student of mainlining, a heavy drinker, thirty-year-old Clancy sat down and shook his head. There were tears in his eyes, but he looked up at me with the last of his altar-boy charm and laughed.

"Hey. How you keep yourself together? When you gonna crack up?"

"Tomorrow or never," I said, then poured two tumblers of wine.

"Ain't that something?"

"That's right, baby."

"No kidding, Charlie. You're together, and I had to see you."

"Here's to the vineyards and the people who toil in them," I said, thinking: At least he doesn't want to borrow money, doesn't need a place to flop for the night.

Clancy shook his head again. "I don't know, sport. I had this gig and was starting to get myself together. I bought some clothes. A TV. Then I start messing round with Martha. Shit. I'm gonna get me some dope."

"Well," I said, sitting down on the unmade bed, "you've had it before. And you're all screwed up. Why not a little dope? Maybe you'll get lucky and get hooked this time."

"Charles," Clancy pleaded. "Don't put the bad mouth on me."

"Did you call your brother?"

"No, but I will." Clancy sighed and filled the tumblers. "You know he's got a cabin up in the mountains, and this fall we could go up there and hunt. Do you good to get out of the city. Maybe you'd like it up there and could write."

Clancy and I did not hunt last fall, nor fish in the spring, but I said, "Yeah. I'd like that. I like the country. Anything to get out of this fucking city."

We had more wine, and Clancy began singing in a

Rex Harrison voice, "California Dreaming," then bolted up and smashed his fist against the wall.

"That bitch. My fucking mother is in California. After Daddy died in prison, she left all of us kids and went to California with a shoe salesman. What kind of mother is that? Don't wanna bring you down, Charlie. Let's have some more wine."

"God said, Let there be light, and there was light," I said.

"You should have been a preacher or a teacher. You're good with kids."

"Yes, my son. Pass the jug."

"You can't destroy yourself, man. You just can't."

"Clancy, I think you've got a point."

"Goddamnit!" Clancy exclaimed, banging his hand on the table, spilling wine. "You can't destroy yourself."

I watched Clancy stagger to the bathroom, staggering like a man trying to avoid a great fire.

The afternoon wine flowed. Cigarette butts filled ashtrays, became tiny smokeless igloos. The hotel was very quiet. The silence was strange, and it seemed to block our conversation as we continued to drink. Once, Clancy choked on wine and cried, "This shit is getting to me, and I'm gonna die. Die and burn in hell."

"Clancy. Take it easy. Feel sleepy?"

"No, man," Clancy said, frowning. "Can't sleep. Have

73

all these terrible dreams. Priests and nuns are coming at me with bull whips, and I have no clothes on."

Sobbing and shaking, Clancy fell to the floor. Pounding his fist he shouted, "Everyone is against me, and they're trying to screw up my mind."

"Oh, shut it, Clancy. You're stoned."

"You nigger bastard. You think you're so fucking, fucking intelligent. So Goddamn cool."

What could I say? I laughed, stretched, yawned, had another wine. This name-calling game bored me. I can live without it. Whitey can't live without it. Without the "games," perhaps we would not be friends: equal in my eyes which you do not acknowledge. Therefore, I am always on my guard. I never know what son-of-bitching trick whitey might pull. My reaction is based on whitey's historical dealing with my people. If that's a poached egg, digest neckbones, chitlings. I know that sooner or later whitey will take a swing at the left nut of my psyche and shout "nigger," in anger, in jest, in sex. At the moment, whitey is trapped on an antique escalator in a building of the future. This is the level where whitey has sunk. With all his power and money.

I left the redheaded, former altar boy on the floor and went up to St. Marks to see what was happening, to bask in the zone of the departing, defeated army of hippies. There used to be a little magic on St. Marks. The black novelist Ishmael Reed calls it hoodoo magic, which means J.W. (jamming whitey). In the Village world of panhandling, the put-down, blacks jam whitey from the center of his emotions to nature's exit. On St. Marks, I met Larl. We had been out of touch and caught up on what had happened: the salt-pork taste of nothing. The mood on St. Marks was calm, almost like the Village in the old days. People sauntered through the speed zone. Up ahead, I spotted a young white man zeroing in on us. Pop-art print shirt, blue jeans. Larl did not see him until he said, "Baby, can you spare a little change?"

Larl turned swiftly, enraged. "Can't you see my face is black, boy! How the hell can I spare anything?"

The healthy boyish charm faded. The young man went away as if he had been punished.

Another small St. Marks encounter. The beggar is a wiry black man who bolted down from a stoop and began rapping with a young man whose face was a map of suburbia. The black man really rapped. Suburbian, Jr., would not release any coins. The black man put his arms around Junior and gave him a peace-movement kiss on the cheek. A few more words and Suburbian, Jr., reached in his pocket and gave the black man a quarter and a dime. The black man told me, "I wish America had another hundred thousand hippies. Then I could make a steady living."

But the fat black hairless queen does not have to worry about a steady living. He is a male nurse, has a sideline hustle. Waddling like a grand female duck, large brilliant eyes, going from left to right, he comes on like a Southern mammy. The queen specializes in young white beggars. "Oh Lord! So many homeless chickens. All they want is a little change or some pot and pills. So they put the make on mother. But I been round since the year one. I take'm to my penthouse on Avenue A. I got plenty of pills, pot, and poppers, and I turns them over faster than you can say eggs and grits. Sometimes they comes back and brings their little long-haired girl friends. And they just all love mother. Oh, my word. Look at that boy crossing that street. What a basket. Well, I must rush off and tend to my chickens." The black queen's dimes, quarters, dollars are a good investment. If a black gives money to whitey, he will be the winner, regardless of what game is being played.

Like Shuffling Joe, who is determined, threatening. Union Square is his base. Union Square is filled with rats; Shuffling Joe has to find "fresh ground." One reason why Shuffling Joe is determined is that he will not drink La Boheme wine, which costs fifty-five cents a pint. "Gallo, man," he says. Gallo is seventy cents a pint. I watch Shuffling Joe hustle a bearded photographer and his lady friend. They are about twenty paces in front of him. The photographer shakes his head, gestures with his hand. His lady friend turns, looks serious; Shuffling Joe watches them move on, still rapping. He grabs the photographer's arm. Photographer grabs camera. Now Shuffling Joe is really rapping, gesturing dramatically. The lady friend has been watching gravely. Suddenly she opens her handbag. A good hustle. Five minutes netted one dollar. "Man," Shuffling Joe says, "I made that cat feel like a turd. I was rapping to him but watching his old lady. I told that cat I was tired. Tired. Tired of fighting whitey and never winning and now all I want to do is drink wine. I can't win 'cause I'm always losing."

This, of course, is a black panhandling truth. We know whitey is still violating our rights as men, as human beings. Whitey is still taking, taking. Even that stuffed rectum of a phrase, RIGHT ON, has reached the portals of the White House. Even the most angelic of white liberals fails to understand black anger, why we react as we do to the most ordinary happenings. Example: window shopping on West Eighth Street, trying to decide if my tight budget would okay an expensive shirt. A bearded white Jesus-type asked for a cigarette.

"Ask your mama," I shouted. In the early hours of morning, I had a pizza on St. Marks. Another white, bearded Jesus-type. This one wanted fifteen cents.

"Motherfucker," I screamed. "I need $5,000."

"Brother," Jesus said, "don't get so uptight."

"Cocksucker," I said, spitting pizza, "I ain't your brother."

I couldn't finish my pizza, suddenly remembering a Connecticut–New York bus trip. My seatmate was young, white, and drank wine. Good Spanish wine. The conversation turned to panhandling. My seatmate was an old St. Marks hand. He had given a black man $15 a few weeks before. I laughed. The boy assured me he would do it again. Indeed! That night the boy (who had made peace with his parents) would go to Kew Gardens, bathe, eat steak ("Ma said . . ."), take the old man's car, pick up his girl, and his buddy and his girl, and buy a pound of grass. Indeed.

But blacks putting the make on other blacks is a cold and colorless story. Even on the Bowery, even when they're sort of on the same wavelength. The "Hey, brother" bit is passé, suspect. The other night a black cat hails me with "Hey, brother. Got a minute to rap?"

"I ain't got shit," I said.

"How you know I want something?"

"Why the hell you stop me, motherfucker?" I asked.

A black and white combo, then? Sometimes this can be very effective, disarming, especially the West Village–St. Marks type. Especially if they're clean and bright as daisies. But what I want to tell you about is a black and white team, a classic encounter. Larl was at Astor Place and Fourth Avenue. Two teen-age girls, one black, the other white, skinny as jay birds in their hip department-store finery. The girls asked Larl for some spare change, Larl ignored them. In unison, the girls shouted, "Cheap cocksucker!"

Larl swung around, marched toward the girls. Then silently raised his hand and, with one powerful stroke, slapped both girls. A crowd gathered. Larl, very aloof, walked away and did not look back. He had to pay $40 to have his watch repaired. A costly street encounter. The games of affluent space-age children, I told a group of supposedly hip hustlers recently. They suggested that I'd make a great panhandler. But panhandling doesn't interest me, just as playing tennis or owning a string of polo ponies doesn't interest me.

LAST NIGHT OPENED tinned sardines. Frequently, opening sardines produces images of hallucinogenic power. It has the feel of a fast "Saturday-night special" (a cheap gun), zipping through that old blasé thing, reality. So I blessed the quart of domestic vodka, bedded on crushed ice in the large Victorian basin. Sardines in tomato sauce. A product of Poland. Sardines tasty, sauce thick, a recession bargain at twenty-nine cents. But do we have a trade agreement with Poland? Cold, iron countries thawing or what the hell, I think, blaming the bad pot. I must read *The News of the Week in Review* in the Sunday *New York Times* and not scan the damn thing.

The vodka is ice cold, delicious. All right then. Three stiff drinks. After working sixteen hours (washing dishes, cleaning up vomit and excrement), I need to unwind. Marat and Sade were the ancestors of my co-workers. The first, second, and third boss? What is there to say about one Jew, one Italian, and one black man? No doubt their mothers loved them. I know their wives do not play the old marriage game. Oh boy! Love is not a dunghill, Hemingway. Love is a 75-caliber machine gun. Another drink and I'll get carried away. In lieu of Beluga caviar (the caterers use supermarket caviar, *pasteurized* caviar, and spoon it out like misers). In lieu of Beluga cavvy, I'm opening another import: smoked sardines from Norway . . . a country that I know very little about except that there is a Lapp tribe in Karasjok. I have a crazy idea that Norway is like California's Orange County. In fact, the vodka just informed me that Norway is exactly like California's Orange County. So conservative that the barks of trees are covered with burlap bags. A country that produced Knut Hamsun, the novelist, and Henrik Ibsen, the playwright, has to be uptight.

The Norwegian sardines have a key opener, which means that I do not have to use my dime-store can opener. Except that I do have to use my opener. The key opener breaks under my muscle-man pressure. I even have difficulty using my own, the tin being soft, so soft that a child could bend it.

I try to make a long cut here and there. Finally, take the stem of my opener and pry the goddamn thing open. Mon Dieu! The tin is smaller than the average bar of soap. But what do you expect for twenty-five cents?

The smoked sardines are a perfect complement for

the vodka. But I'm thinking about the cost of labor, the men or women who fished the sardines out of the sea, the people who packed them, the profits of the Norwegian businessman and the American importer and the Chinese owners of the store where I bought them, and how kind and smiling they are as if I were a new billionaire and had walked into their Knoedler's or Christie's or Parke-Bernet's and said, "Gimme twenty million dollars' worth of art."

Let me lay it on the line: I think progress is simply grand. The chilled vodka agrees. I believe in free enterprise, and hate indifference, cheap products, cheap people, careless people. Two nights ago at Numero Uno, the Pont Royale caterers, the steward, the pantry man forgot the parsley garnish for the prosciutto and melon. With the poise of third-rate comedians, the red-and-green-coated waiters wheeled the carts of prosciutto and melon into the main dining room, for the reception was breaking. Cursing like a nut-ward chorus, they returned to the kitchen with the carts. Dishwashers, bus boys, cooks frantically jerked plastic bags off the parsley, untied strings, snapped stems.

"The parsley hasn't been washed," I said, looking at my wet, dirty hands.

"The parsley hasn't been washed," I protested in a loud voice.

No one answered me. I became frightened and felt

82

like a character in a Kafka novel. Dishwashers, bus boys, cooks, waiters, the steward, the pantry man worked silently and extremely fast. They were putting the final touches on a twenty-five-thousand-dollar wedding party.

The other day, weaving through the East Village, I was accosted by a small black boy about five years old.

"Hey, mister. You got two cents?"

Smiling, I looked down at the boy. "What are you gonna do with two cents?"

"Buy a cookie," the boy replied; his eyes danced darkly. He was very clean; perhaps his mother had just released him from the house.

"Here's a dime, sonny," I said, feeling good. I walked away, skipped a mound of dog excrement, regretting that I didn't have a son. I'd make a great father, friends are always telling me. Unwed mothers, divorcées, widows adjust their antennae of hope, and while I am very fond of these women and their children —they are not the women of future dreams. Maggie? Perhaps. But she is fifteen years older than I am; her womb was always barren. I have no knowledge of fathering children. A romantic rumor of a son in Mexico, that's all.

I looked back at the small black boy. He stood on the corner, counting coins, then approached another man.

I laughed. Clean and bright-eyed. Little black boy. Hustling in the city. Heir Apparent. Crown Prince of Con.

City children are special, seemingly endowed with a knowledge of life, endowed with the knowledge of surviving in the urban jungle while retaining the quicksand innocence and charm of childhood. Once, sitting in cutthroat Chrystie Park, I witnessed a little drama, a scene from a long first act, a lesson in surviving, a lesson for future street gangs. Actions that frequently lead to jail.

I wanted to smoke a joint and walked to the quiet section of the park. A high iron fence enclosed a special area for senior citizens. But that midnight, a group of prekindergarten-age boys had managed to get inside the senior area. They were having a dandy, cursing, rock, wine-bottle, and beer-can battle.

One little boy approached me. "Mister. You'd better watch out. My buddy is gonna throw a bottle over here."

I looked back and ducked in time. A white port-wine bottle zipped through the air, landed at the base of a young tree, where pushers dropped their three-dollar bags of scrambled eggs.

Children are great. Our future. Children are great. Charming little buggers. Especially at midnight. Always midnight. Especially if they are prekindergarten age. Especially if their parents aren't around.

Charles Wright was born in New York City and not New Franklin, Missouri. Charles Wright grew up in the ghetto, joined a gang, which staked out a piece of the turf and took possession of it. A cold Walter Mitty dream? But what takes place in the following dream? No doubt street money and politics would have been involved. A sharp pimp, pusher, addict? There is no doubt in my mind that I would have served time. Perhaps I'd be writing my lawyer, family, friends, asking for books, candy, and cigarettes—instead of writing an entry into a journal.

MOTHERS: California ain't Mississippi. New York ain't Georgia. All offer the same old racial climate. You do not have to go to the heartland of America— say, the Middle West—to take the pollen count of pro-George Wallace sentiments. Simply open the door that fronts on your own back yard. The death of George

Jackson, one of the Soledad Brothers, made me realize that the Auschwitz gates are not closed. They are not awaiting instructions from their superiors. They are waiting to act on their own. Who will be next? Angela Davis? You, me? In Manhattan each day, blacks and Puerto Ricans are roughed up daily before they see a judge or jury. It happens every day to the little people from the urban jungle. Seldom do we hear or read about it.

Sometimes these happenings have the deceptive innocence of childhood, have absolutely nothing to do with drugs, mugging, or even disturbing the peace. It can be nothing more than a handwritten note: "Come for a drink around six. My aunt is coming down and there will be a few other people. Perhaps we'll have dinner. Anyway, please come. They want to meet you." Because I felt guilty for not calling friends, for accepting invitations and never showing, I went to the dinner party, wearing my best suit of depression. Before the hostess offered a drink, she invited me into the kitchen. "I'm so glad you could come. Randy's in the bedroom. I've got to get him out of here before my aunt comes. Could you help me?"

I had a couple of drinks, talked to several pleasant people, then went into the bedroom. Randy's always spaced out. But he was shooting for Zeroville. Since nothing was happening, I said, "Let's split and come back later." But like most schizos, Randy is extremely distrustful. I continued in my opium-saint voice, and we left. In the street, I suggested that we visit an old friend of his, a friend from vocational high school. Randy has a funny little habit of dropping to the floor or sidewalk when he is being advised to do something. He didn't want to see the old high-school buddy. So he fell to the sidewalk about twenty feet from where Wing Ha Sze had been murdered a couple of weeks before. I pleaded with Randy. People stopped, cars slowed. "Old sport," I said, "if you don't get up, I'll have to call the police."

Randy rose like Jesus on the third day. Then we walked down the street, and I bought a couple of Colt 45's. We sat on the stoop of a boarded-up tenement and talked. It was useless. Randy took a swing at me and missed. I took my half-empty can of beer and hit him hard in the corner of his mouth. He fell to the sidewalk.

"Get up," I screamed. "You're making me lose my cool. I'm taking you to Eddie's. I'm tired of trying to help romper-room weaklings."

By the time we reached Grand Street, darkness had set in. Once more, as if following stage directions, Randy fell, between two parked cars. His mouth was bloody. Several curious, long-haired cyclists stopped.

"He's all right." I sighed. "He's only acting."

The cyclists did not believe me. "Listen," I said

angrily, "unless you know something about first aid, you're wasting your time."

Silently, they averted their eyes and drove off. About three minutes later, a tall pale-blond woman and a short dark-haired man with a Thomas Dewey or Hitler mustache stopped. I repeated the story for them. And you know—they didn't believe me. Like an expert rescue team, they picked Randy up and laid him on the sidewalk as I cursed them. Up ahead, two policemen were approaching. The dark-haired man ran to them and said, "Officer, this boy has been hurt."

The two policemen and I went over Randy, who went through his first-day Jesus act.

"What's wrong with him?" a cop asked.

"Nothing," I said. "He's stoned."

"Who hit him?"

"I did. He took a swing at me, and I hit him with a can of beer."

"A full can of beer?"

"Half full."

The policeman searched me, but I was clean as a whistle. And if I never, never had seen hatred before, I saw it in their eyes. Need I tell you, Randy is white and I am black.

The policemen went over to Randy. "Are you all right?" one of them asked.

Randy mumbled. I laughed at the absurdity of it all

and was led toward a building with a nightstick in my back. The cop questioned Randy. He continued to mumble.

"Can't you see he's stoned?" I asked. "There's nothing wrong with him but his head. His old lady left him, and his mother moved and told the neighbors not to give him her new address."

The nightstick-lover of a policeman said, "If you don't shut up, I'm gonna beat you."

Just then a squad car pulled up to the curb. One of the street policemen went to the squad car. The two smiling men in the car had arrested Randy the night before; he had tried to attack a bum with a broken wine bottle. Then they drove off. The cop asked Randy if he wanted to press charges against me. Randy shook his head. The nightstick-loving cop was really angry now. He swung the stick like a demented drum majorette.

The four of us stood on the street corner silently for more than twenty minutes. Apparently the two policemen did not like the end of the happening. Finally, one of them came over to me. Pointing his nightstick down Grand Street, he said, "See those two guys coming this way? One of them has on a red shirt. I want you to start walking in that direction, and don't look back. I don't want to see you in this neighborhood again. I'll lock your ass up."

I walked away, inhaling the absurd Saturday-night air. Later that night, I saw Randy.

"Charles," he said, "I'm sorry. I need help."

I nodded but did not say anything. Mentally I was saying, Come on, feet. Let's make it.

Rain again. Dawn: gray but the light coming through slowly like mother-of-pearl blades on an old windmill. Against the grimy, windowless wall, rippling lines of rain water become an iridescent brick mosaic. Pigeons stir; yawn like grouchy old men. Early subway rumbles, six floors below in the earth, shake the old hotel. My feet want to dance or run.

The morning light expands. A haze evaporates in the room. I dress, go out for *The New York Times,* cigarettes. Return, make tea, eat a cream-cheese-filled bagel. I have decided to read and think about writing again.

Around 10 A.M., finished rereading two favorite Ernest Hemingway short stories: "A Clean Well-lit Place" and "Hills Like White Elephants." Then the phone rang. And although the sky was now fair—it had somehow become black. I will always remember it as a day of silent protest.

SEVENTH AVENUE, NORTH of Forty-second Street. Traffic flowing downtown. The streets are uncrowded at this hour. But the old gray buildings and the old shops with their facelifted fronts are a staunch reminder of the materialistic present—the present of New Yorkers, Ltd. Three Japanese tourists photographed a florist shop, but I looked away and walked toward the Hotel Passover.

The first person I saw in the hotel was Abe Singer, a widowed accountant. He had his fifth-floor door open. An airline bag and camera case were on the bed. Seventy-year-old Abe Singer was in his underwear, drinking a water glass of bourbon as I passed.

"Jamaica, this time," he said, then added, still beaming, "I'm sorry."

The South Carolina maid was a large woman. She looked like an enormous lamp shade in her jungle-print cotton dress. She wore felt houseshoes and always complained of being cold. Age forty, the maid walked beside me, sighing.

"The poor thing," she said. "Sally wouldn't hurt a flea. The police were here, son. Don't touch a thing."

Sally Reinaldo's room was immaculate. A headless Hollywood bed, covered in dark blue satin, was the hub of the room. The turquoise walls were bare as the gleaming wood floor, except for three white fur rugs. Silver-framed photographs of family and friends formed a semicircle on a round table by the bed. But I did not look at them. Green plants in red clay pots crowned a radiator shelf. The venetian blind was closed. I walked over to the dressing table, which had a mirrored top. Perfume, cologne, oils, powder. Bottles and jars—their contents foreign to me. All I knew was that they had something to do with the mystery and magnetism of a woman's face. A wicker tray overflowed with costume jewelry. I shook the tray, listened to the jangling metal sound, then sat down in a slipper chair and smoked a joint. That was when I discovered the overnight bag and the wig box, shiny as black patent leather. The lid had a thin layer of dust on it.

"You really put the icing on the cake this time, baby," I said aloud, and turned on again.

After a while, I could look over at the blue-covered bed, which had dark stains on it.

I could watch memory flash a kaleidoscopic report

from the old world. I saw Sally on West Fifty-seventh Street in May. She had on a black skirt and a white blouse, and I had on a black shirt and white trousers, and we laughed and kissed on the street. Sally asked me to visit her at the Hotel Passover. I promised, but at the time, my social, sexual life was shared only with booze, pills, and pot. Ah, Splendid Solitude! The blessed hours. It is only now that I see the desperation in Sally's eyes, hear that sound in her voice. We had been lovers years ago in Hell's Kitchen. A divorcée, mother of four-year-old-Nelson, Sally wanted to marry me. I was not even wedded to my own budding maturity. We got on damn well together. I remember that if money was tight, she insisted on Nelson and me eating the steak. I remember the Saturday she shopped on Ninth Avenue for food, bought material for a dress, cooked dinner, made the dress and wore it to the opening of Sergi King's Port Afrique on East Sixth Street, just off Second Avenue, in the zone that would become the East Village. Later that morning, Sally and I walked up Second Avenue with Sarmi (a Black Muslim before the great Black Muslim conversion). He had a hard-on for me because I reminded him of a young boy. Mona, a French poet, wanted to offer Sally lesbian love. Mona and Sarmi were friends, and the goodbyes were warm, uncomplicated. But Sally cried before we made love, and in the afternoon, she leaned out the window screaming rape, pelleting a smiling, freckle-face policeman with pecans. In June of that year, I returned to the Lowney Turner Handy Writer's Colony in Marshall, Illinois. Sally made the Las Vegas–Hollywood *la ronde*. It was rumored that she was making $100 a day in Hollywood. No one knew why she returned to New York. No one would ever know. Sally Reinaldo committed suicide on the fifth floor of the Hotel Passover.

I walked all the way back downtown, oblivious to the teeming, early-afternoon streets. Grief, loneliness, self-pity never touched me during the long walk. I simply felt that I had lost something. I opened the door of my hotel room, turned on the radio, drank a beer, showered, and took a sleeping pill. But I couldn't sleep. So I whipped the memory of Sally Reinaldo, who danced a little, sang a little, modeled a little, whored a little, and who wanted to become a star or a housewife, into an olive-green towel and threw it across the room.

Stoned, walking through the early-morning streets, clutching a tumbler of despair. The bars closing. Gradually people appear in the early-morning streets, unsteady in their walk, uncertain of which way to go, what to do. The full white moon, stationary, like a man-made object flung into space, like a flag announcing,

"We have arrived. We have set foot on the floor of your dead planet."

And it seemed to me that the street people were tourists on that dead planet. Against their will, they had detoured from the route of dreams. Frightening, oblique loneliness became the fellow traveler. But there was nothing I could do about it. I felt that I had left part of my insides in Sally Reinaldo's fifth-floor room at the Hotel Passover. I considered myself extremely lucky. A practical man, I gave up Waterloo and concentrated on exile. New York. Hades-on-the-Hudson. It is time to take leave of it. But for the moment, I am comforted with nothing but the prospect of another sunrise, buried in my own mortality.

On the Bowery, bells do not toll. But cocks crow at the Shangwood Live Poultry Market, and sincere hymns blare from the two Bowery Salvation Army havens, pleading with the classless, transient army of men to come unto God. And it seems to me that they should try Him or seriously think about hitting the road. Urban renewal is upon them. A broom is all that is needed for these powerless, nonpolitical men. (Most of them believe they are part of the political scene, hard-hatted in their wine stupor.) "The Bowery will never change," one of them told me recently. "I should know. I've been here twenty-five years."

The Bowery has been changing for a very long time. And there was nothing subtle about the change. Three years ago, non-AIR residents were evicted from lofts, small businesses were forced to move. The raunchy bar called Number One, between the Bowery and Second Avenue, was the first to go, then the Blue Moon. Betty's became the chic circus-yellow front. The pissoir-rich old Palace bar is now Hilly's, where an old-timer rapped on the door one early dawn, like a Scott Fitzgerald ghost in "Babylon Revisited," and asked hoarsely, "Is Jimmie still here?" The legendary Horse Market restaurant folded, replaced by the Bowery Coffee Shop, which also folded. The hotels are going, gone. The Boston, the Clover, the Defender. But what soured hearts was the closing of Sammy's Bowery Follies, although few winos were Follies customers. It was a symbol like the White Horse, the Lion's Head, St. Adrian's, and Max's Kansas City.

Now live rock blares on the Bowery. There are elegant living lofts, waiting only for *House Beautiful*'s photographer or *Vogue* magazine and art galleries. Now local color is provided by the affluent children of Aquarius with their frizzed hair, dirty jeans, and expensive, scuffed boots, and their dolls with their frizzed hair and 1930's style of dressing and their talk of pot, peace, and pollution. They are as cold and capitalistic as the parents they fled. To them the bums are a nuisance. They lack the old bohemian feeling of togetherness. As one tall, bearded artist said to me, "Hell, I've told you about sitting on my stoop. I got an old lady and kids."

All the winos have is each other and the Capital of Pluck (wine). The Capital of Pluck is the Municipal Lodging House for Men on East Third Street, which throughout America's wine world is called "the Muney." Only in the city of New York are these men able to breathe. The Muney will secure free rooms at Bowery hotels, plus three decent meals a day. With the advent of the Nixon regime's phase-in, phase-out, the Muney is uptight. Even the annual Muney summer riots failed to materialize. (The parent group drifted away, got busted, went to the Catskills to work. The main man had severe drug hallucinations.)

On the Bowery, drugs are running a close second to wine. Especially with young blacks and Puerto Ricans. Indeed, Eugene O'Neill's Iceman would come down to the Bowery looking for a fix.

Like New York night life, business is off in the bars, although men are sitting at the tables before the official 8 A.M. opening. But they sit all day, trying to hustle drinks like pitiful old whores, like shameless clowns.

Sitting and waiting for the silent mushroom in the

sky, watching the desperate jackrollers, who in turn are watching them. Money is tight. A daytime robbery is a common happening. Most of the older men try to make it back to the hotels before darkness sets in or go in pairs, groups.

There are no black bars on the Bowery. The blacks prefer to drink on street corners, which is cheaper. There are hotels that will not rent rooms to blacks, and there are hotels which have separate but equal floors for blacks and whites, although both use the same bathrooms. The wine climate of the Bowery has always been racial. This has not changed. The majority of these weak drinking men come from the primeval American South. Wine has not shrunk their racial war; it has enlarged it to the point of fanaticism. Ethnic to the last pint of La Boheme white port (the most popular brand), the mix is roughly Irish and blacks running neck and neck, followed by Poles. There are few Italians, Jews, Chinese. But keeping pace with the national cultural explosion, increasing numbers of young men are nestling in the ruins. Most of them are very hip, according to the old-timer's social register.

The story goes that the police are tougher on white winos than on blacks. Whites are superior and shouldn't sink to that dark level. But it is only the old black men who retain the hairs of *machismo*. Before sunrise, black and white men are in the streets, walking up and down like women on market day, like desperate junkies. At that hour they are waiting for the early-morning "doctors," peddling illegal wine. Illegal wine is now $1.25 a pint. Yet the men who sleep in their own urine on the sidewalk and wipe car windows with dirty rags manage to pay the "doctor," just as more affluent Americans manage to have charge accounts.

For these Bowery men are American, too, with that great American dream. Tomorrow we will seek a new design for living, new territories, which is why the Bowery has expanded into little Bowery zones. The main zone is the Greenwich Hotel on Bleecker and the Lady Jane West, both old zones. If it were not for the drugquake, the press, and law-and-order citizens, very few people would be aware of the zones. The Keystone Hotel in midtown, one block from Macy's, has been operating for a long time, and the winos have Herald Square, Bryant Park. Another group of winos operates exclusively on Forty-second Street. From the Port Authority, the junction being Grant's Cafeteria and the end of the rich line, Grand Central. Now they've made it down to Wall Street and up to Central Park and the chic East Side streets. Many of the new buildings have openings where a man can seek shelter from the rain or cold. Just for a night.

But then bums have always been transient, always on the move, returning to their home which has always been there, even if only in the mind. The artists will go, too, in time, just as the winos are going. And although Kate Millett may be liberated and celebrated, she, too, will go.

The Bowery is a cinema museum in hell where classic films play forever. Occasionally, selected shorts play, are spliced together, and become classics themselves. And although I still visit the Bowery, there is nothing more to learn. Ravished by their own weakness and the conditions of American life, Bowery men have their Grand Hotel and are content. But other men are attracted to the Bowery because of laziness. All they want to do is drink and shoot the breeze. I hope you realize that is the entire frame for the Bowery.

The Chinese say that the first step is the beginning of a ten-thousand-mile journey. But what is the first step?

At the end of the Bowery, there is Chinatown and the Chinese Garden.

Once almost as remote as a desert fortress, my Chinese Garden, my *bête noire,* is a symbol of the goose-stepping '70's. Sometimes I think nature, man, space-age progress are conspiring to build a terrible corrupt monument for the year 2001. Can this be true? Or have I been on the downward path as far as my fellow human beings are concerned? But once my garden was my church. Layered in concrete, the cesspool of greenery rises at its highest level about thirty feet where the Bowery and Canal meet to channel traffic to Brooklyn and elsewhere. Motorists consider it an unexpected, delightful slice-of-life landscape. Soon it will become a mini-tourist attraction.

Recently, a group of young black, white, Puerto Rican, and Chinese artists set up shop between the hours of eleven and three, painting pop designs on all surfaces except dirt and grass. Against the weathered gray of concrete, black silhouettes. A prisoner hanging from his cell. Two Afro heads in a heavy chess game. And from the old world, stencil designs of Chinese dragons. Although I applaud their slow, sincere efforts, this is of no value to me. All I know is my garden has been invaded by people who represent the blowup of New York. People arrive, perform, depart. Countless variations on an urban theme. These people make police reports, signal, Bellevue, Kings County, pay the bread man of drugs. These people confront policemen, merge with the winos and the goldbricking Department of Parks workers, the artistic elite from the neighboring lofts and the Chinese immigrants, who instantly, magically, accept the American middle-class outer garment. You see, I am the senior citizen of the garden. Six years, day and night, summer and winter—I have sat on that stone ledge, surrounded by thirty-nine trees, watching people arrive like ghosts in a real dream.

Except for the long stone ledges, there is nothing. The playground equipment has been removed. The toilets have been sealed for eternity in concrete. All that remains are the ledges, trees, and elegant lampposts. Most of the time, only a few lamps are lit. The other night, four teen-age boys marched through the garden and surveyed the scene. Then three of the boys ran out of the garden. The fourth boy returned. He walked through the garden like a Midwestern basketball star before a county championship. But his turf was urban. Stone under those imitation French cycling shoes. His hand was steady as he shot out all the lights. And in the semidarkness the boy looked over at me and smiled. I saluted him. Hadn't I reported him to the police (at their request) before? Once, surrounded by a gang, I cleverly signaled to a policeman. He knew that the boys were throwing bottles and rocks into the street, had hit a woman with a baby and had broken the window of a Ford station wagon.

And of course, there are the dogs. People unleash their dogs; smile proudly as if they had conceived them on some passionate, dark night. Their eyes never leave the dogs, even when they defecate on the grass where winos sleep, children play, young lovers love. It is very sad. The dog owners appear to be sane, intelligent, well dressed. The artistic types are fashionably disheveled.

The saddest scene that I encountered in the Chinese Garden was not the murder of Wing Ha Sze, nor a very masculine wino serving head at high noon. No, it was a fat, laughing Chinese girl about three years old. Even today, I can see the girl's parents' mood shift from pride to horror. Sunlight through the full-leafed trees, gleaming on the pale blue satin hair ribbons, the blue-and-white gingham dress. The laughing girl began running and fell to the ground. A rich image of dog excrement colored her bosom like a Jim Dine valentine.

I can also see three mothers and four children picnicking on the grass. It was late August. A humid afternoon. The pollution count was high, and traffic cried, crawled across Manhattan Bridge. I locked my mental camera at 5:10, according to the clock in the parking lot on Bayard Street. Opened another King Rheingold, content with the world around me and the world out there. That is, until a half-ass domestic French poodle tried to dry-fuck one of the children, a boy about four years old. The three mothers, elegantly balancing cigarettes and bottles of Miller High Life in their hands, might have been figures in a Bonnard landscape.

But the screaming small boy's fear brought me back into the present. I finished my beer and watched the horny dog mount another child, a toddling tot, a boy still a little uneasy about what was underneath his feet. The excited dog knocked the boy to the ground. The dog's tongue flapped as if dying of thirst. The laughing mothers continued to smoke and drink beer.

I stood up, looked north through the arches of Manhattan Bridge, through the pollution screen toward the Empire State Building, then south toward the old buildings of Chinatown, sitting on a real-estate dish of excellent sweet pork. The cubistic Chatham Towers rise above them. With soot powdering their historic façades, municipal New York and Wall Street overpower them. However, new buildings such as the World Trade Center rise above history, as if to embrace the sky. In Chatham Square, chained to a young tree, three metal chairs proclaim JESUS SAVES.

But there are eighteen broken parking meters in my garden, like the end of a rip-off happening of abstract sculpture. Drug addicts, functioning as human jackhammers, carried them up from the streets between midnight and dawn. I arrived at 6 A.M. with coffee, the Sunday *New York Times*, and thought: Where are the police, the concerned citizens? Indifference might have a past. Am I right in assuming that it has a future?

Of late, small armies of policemen (usually Chinese,

with a couple of novice Wasp detectives) march through my garden on a groping, fascist search. But there is no one except me, two young lovers, and the winos. Open, open! There is no place to hide. Frequently, New York's finest question me, their hands roughly moving from the top of my head to my feet. Then, apparently unsatisfied, they flash their brilliant flashlights in my face. This does nothing for them. So they turn the flashlights up into the thirty-nine trees. And as they walk toward the Bayard Street exit, I ask if I can help them. Their voices, like their eyes, are elsewhere. You see, New York's finest say they are simply on a routine patrol, which is a goddamn lie. I am the senior citizen of the Chinese Garden, the resident historian, the wild-grass accountant. I also do extra duty outside of the garden. Within a ten-block radius of the garden, I am familiar with crime and corruption. Therefore, I hope no one will be foolish enough to think the rise in crime has anything to do with the police's presence in my garden.

The sentry knows who patrols the desecrated island of concrete and trees. Just the other day, a daring group of British tourists marched into the garden. The excitement of discovery seemed to color their voices and eyes. A Byzantine ruin, or a secret Persian Garden? Here, marijuana, wine, baseball outrank young love and volleyball. Here, the sons of Chinese immigrants are becoming skilled American baseball players. Dressed in red, the Free Mason volleyball team plays an excellent game, lacking only American competitive drive. Their game is passive, as if volleyball were programmed and, chop—a programmed karate class, still working out at a quarter of nine in the evening.

The sky had not turned dark, and I watched the teacher and his male and female assistants. There was something uncomfortable about their voices and mannerisms. I tried not to think of the future of the mixed racial bag of ghetto students. No matter, no matter. Strange green thumbs are cultivating young plants here. I repeat: no matter, no matter—all of these people are in no way part of my garden. I do not regret their invasion. No, I regret America's invasion into the porous walls of their minds.

But the Cat Woman is the most radiant human being I encountered in the Chinese Garden. She arrived one afternoon in the summer of 1970, looking like a thrift-shop visionary, moving as if her yellow-shod ballerina feet were monitored by snails. The Cat Woman bowed toward the volleyball players in the former playground. Ah! She smiled—waltzed under the full-leafed trees that were like a roof. Presently I could see her lips move. Now and then, the Cat Woman held her hands above her eyes, then walked to the center of the garden. You could say the center is a cross. (The center has four squares of greenery.) Anyway, the Cat Woman prayed briefly, then stood between two trees and raised her arms toward the watercolor sky; then apparently passion seized her. She fell to the ground and began clawing in the dry earth with her hands, trying to dig up the beloved cat she had buried there the year before. More than a dozen people were in the garden that afternoon, and without talking to any of them, I discovered that the Cat Woman's father, and then her nine-year-old daughter, had failed to give her enough love. The dead cat, "He was so nice." Life was a soufflé without him.

Almost a year later, I thought I saw the Cat Woman. I was going home, taking the tourist route through Chinatown. I stopped at the clam house which is across the street from the garden. The moon was full. City lights glowed. The neon veneer of Chinatown created a rainbow haze. But the woman I saw was more than sixty feet from where I stood popping clams. Almost at the top of the second entrance's steps, where the trees began and where the light is dim. I ran toward the woman like a man possessed with a vision.

Indeed, it was the Cat Woman. She was blessed with a vision. She knew that someone would enter the deserted garden and ask her a question. Her young daughter was fine. But mothers and fathers were out this year, she said.

107

"The cat," she exclaimed, offering me a drink from a Hiram Walker pint. "You remember. Well, I've got good news for you. He came back to life, and I'm so happy."

Was there a time when a once dead, now live cat, or a child with a balloon, would have startled me in the Chinese Garden? Yes, there was a time. It was during the early stage of the Great Society.

LIKE MOST MEN, the Chinese prefer foreign sexual hors d'oeuvres, and there are many Occidental whores in Chinatown. But whorehouse hotels do not exist. Dollar-sign sex takes place in cars, in door entrances on dark, deserted business streets, or in hotels near the Bowery. Recently, encounters have taken place in the Chinese Garden. Miss Nell from Dallas, Texas, works here. An exceptionally large woman, Miss Nell appears to be powdered from head to foot with white chalk dust. She looks like a visitor from a country where there is no sunlight. Strawberry-blond ringlets circle her wide pleasant face. Her voice is like a tiny rusty bell. Extremely sensitive about her size and profession, Miss Nell will exit from a taxi as if taking the first steps to the funeral of a beloved friend. By the time she has planted her feet on the sidewalk, she has become the sultry, shrewd businesswoman and moves slowly, like a great, proud queen, her bell-like voice a litany of love for sale.

Shortly before 8 P.M. one night, Miss Nell arrived in the Chinese Garden with a customer. Standing under a Victorian lamppost, she surveyed the garden like a field marshal. Two young lovers sat with their dog near the former playground.

Miss Nell, wearing a sensational black-and-white mini dress and white sandals (a pair of 1940 Joan Crawford "fuck me" shoes), motioned to the nervous man to follow her. She held a large white handbag, white gloves, a clear plastic umbrella decorated with white flowers in her right hand. A perfect Fellini whore, she moved through the tall grass toward a large tree about fifteen feet from where I sat. The man, who had his hands in his pockets, followed at a fast pace.

Still clutching the white bag, gloves, umbrella, Miss Nell went through the ritual of going down on the man. She worked very hard. She worked with great feeling. She worked like a professional. Miss Nell worked for a very long time. Now and then, she'd look up at the man, and you could almost read her mind. Finally, she stood up, lifted her skirt, and offered her buttocks. This did not help the man, who was now working very hard. Miss Nell decided to try the door of life. Still clutching the bag, umbrella, gloves, she put her large arms around the man. She might have been a mother comforting a small child. But Miss Nell and the man moved with great passion. He was very relaxed and even smiled. He did not reach a climax.

Exhausted, Miss Nell led the man over to the ledge where I was sitting. The man smiled and joked. Miss Nell was angry. She looked down at me, opened the clear plastic umbrella with the pretty white flowers on it, and tried to block my view. It was like trying to cover the Empire State Building with a single bed sheet.

Once more the hard-working professional went down on her customer. And I thought they would make it this time. But Miss Nell jumped up and screamed, "My God! What's wrong with you? I ain't got all night. I've got to take care of business."

The man was still smiling and asked for a two-dollar refund.

Miss Nell snapped open her white handbag and said, "With pleasure." Then she walked out of the garden swiftly, her head down like an unhappy queen. The man followed at a distance.

Then the young lovers, who are almost nightly visitors, rose and walked out of the Chinese Garden, the small auburn dog running ahead of them, his metal leash hitting the pavement dully, sounding as I imagined Miss Nell would sound with a very bad cold.

*A profound statement from a country-club divorcée,
age forty-two. A former secretary, the divorcée had
also worked in advertising and public relations. It was
almost midnight, and the tranquilizers and Scotch had
failed to extinguish the lady's anger: "Hell. People think
alimony is easy. I worked sixteen years for that money.
And when it runs out, I'll become a whore. Men love
whores. I know. Lennie married a bona fide whore."*

The symposium, "Toward the Elimination of Prostitution," reminded me of—say—the Ku Klux Klan in
Iceland: absurd. The Babbitt sisters of Salem, Massa-
chusetts, or simply a confused but sincere movement
of sisters? Even the together women writers such as
Susan Brownmiller were caught in the breeze that
whispered Joseph McCarthy. The good, "straight,"
middle-class white women should go underground like
the Weathermen and produce an anti-prostitution pill,
force chastity belts on the men they live with, or get
married. Even an occasional lay would help. And although I'd vote for improving the female condition,
I'm depressed by these hen-pecked solutions to the
female-male misunderstanding. Depressed, depressed.
It's like trying to ejaculate inside a vagina the size of
the entrance to the Holland tunnel.

In a symbolical and a real sense, slavery hasn't been
formally abolished in the United States. But the ma-

jority of women who become prostitutes do so of their own free will. It seems like easy work and fast money. I refuse to subscribe to the women's movement's use of prostitutes as a Salvation Army cause. The propaganda oozes emotional perfume. The shtick is a roadrunner of a masculine Madison Avenue campaign. How effective will such a campaign be in our time? The good women stated it beautifully: "The topic, if allowed to be openly discussed, would have reached to the roots of our sexual fears and fantasies . . ." Ours is a perilous voyage. There is the uneasy knowledge that it might be our last; the harbor hasn't been sighted. We could drown. How stupid of us! Why can't we redesign the lifeboats, take a good hard look at our male-and-female relationship? Perhaps redefine sin, morality, and corruption for our time on this earth.

The baptism of a whore is the acceptance of a pimp's psychological rap. After this ritual, the "straight" woman becomes a whore and the pimp's bank. If one rap fails to convince the "straight" woman, then the pimp will use another rap. Most pimps are not great lovers or handsome in the movie-star sense. I know a black, middle-aged pimp who is five feet tall and looks like a frog. Whores dig the man. They give him money, and he buys their clothes. All of them seem to be content with the arrangement. Recently I saw the pimp on

Fourteenth Street. He had his arms around two of his girls, and all of them were smiling, and they might have been rehearsing for a 1980 television commercial.

"Would you whore?" I asked a young actress who had worked briefly at a whore bar.

"No."

"Why?"

"No moral reason. I just wouldn't enjoy the work." But like most women, the actress found the whore-pimp scene fascinating. "I can understand how straight women fall for it. Especially emotionally insecure women. The rap is beautiful. Reassuring. If straight men used the rap of a pimp, male and female relations would improve."

"Would you make me whore?" Kitty asked.

The words jammed against my Protestant shelter. But my male ego tripped. Kitty would whore for me. She would do anything for me. All in the name of love.

"If it were profitable for both of us." I laughed and took her to bed. Our relationship was warm, uncomplicated. We never mentioned whoring again. But a month later, Kitty told me that she had a dinner date at the Waldorf Astoria (Count Basie had just opened). The following afternoon, Kitty gave me $50 to buy food. She was an excellent cook. Mentally, the dinner that night lacked flavor. Of course, I could have got stoned, beat up on Kitty, and put her down or rapped about the fabulous Waldorf, then changed gears and, ever so sincere, rapped about a poor, uptight writer who loved her. That's it: there's nothing else to know. Kitty was an occasional whore, and it brought her little joy, although I believe she enjoyed it in a subconscious sense: it was degrading.

Last year, a twenty-year-old addict asked me if I would take money from her. I needed money, and she wanted to help me. I was for real. Hadn't I from the very beginning respected her? I had never put her down, *made her feel like dirt.*

There are a variety of trees in the prostitution forest. My friend's wife doesn't enjoy oral sex, but tries to go along with the program. My friend, the father of two children, loves his wife. They have been married for eight years. A mistress would definitely complicate their relationship. The husband, father, lover, friend has whores orally.

And oh, you earthshaking movement sisters! What about the boys in Vietnam? Your countrymen, husbands, brothers, lovers, and friends. As they wait to kill or be killed, would you deny them one of life's greatest pleasures? Would you want them to use five fingers? As a former army man, I want to tell you this: I put my young life on the line for you. I helped build roads, schools in Korea. I gave my time and money to those poor people. I hate to think of all the women and children who might have starved without some Korean woman selling her body for an hour, a night, or a month. To relieve the fear of the uneasy truce, boredom, and petty politics of barracks (tent) life, there was nothing else a man could do but get stoned and screw. Or use five fingers, abstain, or—a sign in an army john: FINCH WOULD DO IN A PINCH.

Prostitutes forever! Long live the golden girls of the streets!

I'm for legalizing prostitution. Suspicious of the women's movement's motives in their anti-prostitution drive. Afraid of competition? Outlawing prostitution gives "straight" women an advantage. But I doubt if it brings women and men together on an equal level of understanding, desire, and need.

THE EAST VILLAGE worms its way through a Ponce de León garden of drugs. But flowers dry, die. In the sun, in a musical cigarette box on a glass-top coffee table, in an oven, and, fenced in a newspaper blanket (limp as pizza dough), on a radiator. A *Reader's Digest* of scents, offering the fresh air of peace of mind or a hallucinating high.

Journeying into the interior of Welfare-Drugsville, where the last of the flowers were in the final stage of exile, I remember the sparse summer trees seemed unreal: models for Madame Tussaud's wax museum. In a ten-block area I encountered no police. The streets were monitored by junkies, thieves, pushers, a new breed of whores who sipped iced Cokes and coffee in the heat of afternoon. Domesticated hippies walked Doberman pinschers, German shepherds, or fashionable mongrels, while black and Puerto Rican teenagers, natives of "East Village" (the Lower East Side), motherfuck each other with words. The ancient tenements are monuments to the splendor of welfare. The poor, the uneducated are powerless against the government's yearly rape. Even whores get tired. Model tenements in Utopia! In lieu of flowers, garbage litters the pavement. Car arson is a big sport in the East Village (two cars in three days on East Eleventh Street between Avenues B and C). The fire department and police daily offer their services.

Social workers, VISTA (*vision*) workers, the Church offer services. Nothing changes. The old woman who laughs like an exhausted mare is still inspecting garbage cans, a Horn & Hardart shopping bag wreathed over her arm. A stringbean junkie, age twenty, has been stealing something almost daily for two years.

You see I am no stranger here. "You know all of those people over there," Shirley had said. "Please see if you can find Denise."

Denise had split from the pad on Ninth Street. The R.O.T.C. student had split. The last member of the party, a blonde, a chocolate-chip cookie of a girl, was alone and depressed; the rent was due. As I waited for the elevator, two junkies tried to sell me a pair of ice skates. Toto Thomas has worked many scenes: reform school, Golden Gloves, con artist, armed robbery, file clerk, messenger, truck driver. Then he blossomed into a blue-eyed flower and sat in Tompkins Square like a human rocket waiting for the countdown. Where was Denise? Well—

"Man. It's good to see you. And you know something? I'm gonna make it this time. I've got a good scene uptown. But I'm gonna make it down here once in a while."

We went over to the pad Toto Thomas had crashed and shared with four pleasant, apple-cheeked young men from suburbia. The pad was neat like a college dormitory. The young men were leaving. They were very careful with their garbage. I watched them force bulging paper bags into a garbage can and then replace the lid. Four well-mannered young men who for the moment controlled heroin like conservative stockbrokers.

"I don't shoot any more," Toto Thomas said. "Just baby shots. Water shots." Toto picked up wads of cotton which contained heroin dregs. Just before shooting up, he turned to me and grinned. "Now I'm ready to rap and go out and get a piece. Ball, baby. That's what I always say."

The same afternoon, I met Peter on Avenue B. "Where you been?" he asked. "You look bad. Are you still looking for that pet? Wanna couple of pills? I got pills, baby. Pills to go to bed with. I'm back with my old lady and *her* girl friend."

A boy who appeared to be about sixteen years old

walked up. Peter made a sale. Then the boy turned to me. Without blinking an eye, he asked, "You wanna get rimmed?"

"No," I said. "That bores me."

The three of us laughed. The boy started off, walking like an ambitious executive. At least the last of the flower children were interested in the pollen count. Anything goes! The New World's sexuality! Lord, sometimes I ask myself, Are they for real, are they free? Rimming, once a whispered desire of sexual swingers, is slowly surfacing from down under. And it seems somehow appropriate to mention human excrement and cannibalism as mankind prepares not to scale the summits but to take the downward path into the great valley of the void.

Thoughts pinballed through my mind; the questionnaire was almost blank, and I stopped off at Sam's; he lives in one of those medieval wrecks. The last of the communal flowers were limp in front of the building. They sat on the stoop, played guitars, sang on fire escapes, and got high on stairwells, seemingly placed there by a landscape architect, schooled in James Joyce's Nighttown.

Miss Ohio manned the second floor. Glowing with warmth, she had just returned from visiting her parents and giggled about her new silver-buckled shoes. Miss Ohio had been on the scene for almost a year. Nothing bad had happened to her—yet. Occasionally she gets high, talks about being "hung-up" on some "cat," spends most of her time with the neighborhood children. She seems so out of place in the East Village. She belongs to the world of babies, chintz-flowered bedrooms, country kitchens.

On the third floor, I had to step over a group of stoned children. Sam was talking with—let's call him Jerry. Sam works in Jerry's uncle's midtown office. We sat around listening to records, getting high. Then the white chick from upstairs arrived. She's got a Jones, a thing for black dudes. A hefty girl with a ban-the-bomb air. Her old man had split, and she wanted Sam to help her find him. "The bastard is probably in Washington Square because he knows I don't hang out there."

Meanwhile, longhaired Jerry had placed his booted feet on the lower shelf of the coffee table, his elbows rigid on his knees.

"I don't wanna cry," he whimpered. But he made no effort to check the tears. "I can't stand it. Last summer I was flipping out. Speed and every goddamn thing. Paranoid as a son of a bitch, and one night these punk kids tried to jump me. They were high, too. On pot and wine. I wasn't trying to cop a plea. I just didn't wanna fight. I started to run, and one of them comes after me. I gave him a belt in the stomach, and he fell back and hit his head against one of those old-fashioned stoops."

Jerry bolted up from the sofa. "I just can't stand it. I'm dreaming about it all the time. His mother—she was holding his head. 'You killed my son.' Now I don't take anything. Drink booze, smoke a little pot. I'm on probation, and the family and everyone treats me with kid gloves. But I don't feel free."

Later, suffering Death Valley Days of the mind, Jerry was crawling on the floor, crying, beating his fists against the floorboards.

I looked out the window. On the roof across the street, a sailor on leave drank a quart of Miller High Life and looked down at the street scene. A civilian last summer, he was always on the roof at dawn. Alone in the early summer quiet, then he drank cans of Rheingold, ranted and raved at the young people who balled and slept on the roof opposite him. His roof was one story higher than the Drugsville roof. I remember that he was like an angry Baptist preacher. A frustrated, beer-drinking, Saturday-night hard hat. Perhaps the navy had been very good for him. Perhaps he had matured and from the experience had become a man, had gained confidence and had had women. Perhaps his I-am-at-peace-with-the-world had crystallized because flowers no longer blossomed and balled on rooftops. I'll never know. I sensed he wanted to talk to me.

But I turned from the window. It had been a long trip. Darkness was a long way off. The hip and beautiful flowers were dead, out of season, waiting to be reincarnated and given a new name, a new scene.

You know how it is. Memory quivers like a vibrating machine, and you smile. "Golly, Miss Molly."

I had been drinking in the White Horse with two of my more stable earthlings. A nine-to-five Literary Chap in a Chipp suit. His companion was a down-in East Village boutique girl. They wanted me to go with them to a Hotel Albert party. But I remembered too many roller-coaster days, nights, schlepping early-morning ghosts, hallucinating rock revivals at the priceless Albert. So I made it across town and went to the Old Dover in the Bowery. In this frantic bag of hell, I could be absolutely alone. The regulars, stoned on cheap wine, respected my privacy. I had trained myself against the babbling voices around me. I would play "Hey Jude" and "Revolution," knock down vodka, and make it. Sitting at my customary station at the bar, turned toward the street, I watched a chic *Harper's Bazaar* type of girl saunter in. She was Lady Brett Ashley, stoned on salvation.

"You weak bastards," she shouted. "Get back into the mainstream of life!"

The jukebox swung with "Can I Change My Mind and Start All Over Again?" The Bennington girl, masquerading as Lady Brett, wanted to dance. A real nigger type, carried away by the promise of the moment, asked me for a cigarette. "If you can't make it without a smoke, you're nowhere," I told him.

Meanwhile, the sotted sister threw her handbag on the bar and winked at me. A game, a happening, no matter, no matter. I knew her kind and gave her my Rover Boy smile. Lady Brett began dancing alone. A parody of a sensual grind. Surrounded by stoned but reserved men, she had for the moment forgotten her mission of soul-saving. But the bartender, followed by his henchmen, threw Our Lady of the Bowery, kin of Hemingway and *Harper's Bazaar*, out the door. No one followed the lady's exit.

A dark, port-wine-drinking young man came up to the bar. Despite the warm night, he carried a leather jacket and had on black bell-bottoms, black T-shirt, and Swiss-hi shoes (in other words construction-worker high tops. Laces of tan leather, Dupont neoprene crepe soles. These shoes are extremely popular for comfort and durability, and offer the weight of a coffee cup's illusion of masculinity. In fact, knowledgeable people call them "fruit boots").

"Wanna smoke from a dead man?" Leather Jacket asked, offering a hand-rolled cigarette.

I accepted and discovered a man had died in the bar earlier. Men are always passing out, sleeping on the tables and floor, and the dead man was, well—on the floor. All Leather Jacket knew was that the cops went through the man's pockets, searching for identification. They laughed and joked with the regulars. A cop had given Leather Jacket the dead man's tobacco and cigarette papers.

Leather Jacket ordered two dark ports, before confession. Once again, I am working on my sainthood: I listen. A Catholic, another cross in the seemingly endless line of raunchy souls I've encountered recently: Czechs, Poles, Irish, Italians, and Puerto Ricans. Guilt works overtime for them. I'm not sure if they want help or simply want to recharge their emotional batteries. But Catholic youth is the victim of their passion, frustration, and hatred. Apparently family and Church have failed these weak men. Unable to recognize their latent disturbances, they simply hustle them down the medieval road of morality and guilt. Any intelligent child questions that road, especially if it detours from the reality around him.

"My old lady put me out," Leather Jacket was saying. "I lost my job and left Jersey City. I've been drinking since Easter."

"You seem to be doing all right," I said.

"Well, I got cleaned up. You should have seen me last week."

A small black queen, sitting ringside, graciously accepts the good nights of the courtly regulars. Makes it with a lean hillbilly escort.

"My old lady looks something like that." Leather Jacket laughed.

"Do you mean she's black and ugly, or a man?" I asked.

Leather Jacket looked directly at me and smiled. "I guess you got the scene figured out."

"I don't know," I said, ordering another vodka. Leather Jacket opened the cage of his past. An American Catholic Classic in some respects. Hard-working, hard-drinking father died when Leather Jacket was an altar boy. Mom ("A beautiful broad, I wanted to make it with her. I think she wanted to make it with me, too") put her two sons and three daughters in an orphanage and shopped around for a new husband. Mom eventually married a rich old man and moved to Montreal. The children remained in the orphanage. Leather Jacket rebelled against the sadistic fathers and nuns. "It fucked with my psyche, but I'm sort of together."

Enlisting in the army, Leather Jacket continued his personal revolt. "Nothing has ever been able to break me." After a medical discharge, he worked in factories, diners, gas stations. A black schoolteacher stopped for gas one day and propositioned Leather Jacket. "I remember following her up the steps. Man. He was big and ugly, but I sort of dug him. Weird man."

"And there were red lights in the pad, and he called you Daddy."

"You're a smart son of a bitch. You got the whole fucking scene figured out."

"I'm not putting you down," I said. "But I've heard the story before."

Leather Jacket's brain was at the bottom of the wine barrel. "I'm all fucked up," he said, breathing hard. "I get so goddamned tired and lonely, and it's not all sex, you know. Hell. I could have almost any broad I want, and you know about the queens."

I understood, thinking: Jesus. I hope he doesn't start the waterworks. Leather Jacket was more honest than most twenty-five-year-olds from his prison. I remembered a Spanish queen who lived nearby. Her old man had left for P.R. The queen was alone and lonely. Perhaps Leather Jacket and the Spanish queen could, at least for the night, quench their loneliness. As we departed, I wondered where was my saintly halo, my recluse's cabin by the sea.

Coco gave Leather Jacket her Park Avenue welcome. We went into the living room. All the major pieces of furniture were covered in custom plastic, including the fluffy 9-by-12 white cotton rug. The art objects were holy: gilt madonnas with rosebud halos. Jesus Christ was everywhere. Plastic, coppertone, brass plate, plaster of Paris. The room was heady with orange blossom refresher. Large votive candles created a mood appropriate for a wake, séance or Mass. Coco and Leather Jacket made small talk while I looked over the record collection. Already, I could sense they would work something out and that it would go well for them. I put on an LP, smoked a joint, very happy about the whole scene. Then Pepe, the ex-husband, lumbered in from the bedroom, yawning. He greeted me warmly and shook hands with Leather Jacket, and I knew that they would be enemies.

But Coco was in his glory. An amused queen enthroned in a red Easy Boy lounge chair. Pepe showed me the long knife he had bought on Forty-second Street. Leather Jacket was an excellent knife thrower. Coco cooed and teased. Pepe and Leather Jacket fought for his favors. Then Coco invited me into his neat little kitchen. He thanked me, and I inhaled Avon's Fandango perfume.

"Forget it, doll."

"He came back and I took him back, but I'll show him tonight."

The night danced on and on. We got higher. Pepe and Leather Jacket remained on guard. Coco remained on the throne. The three non-jazz lovers seemed to enjoy the records I played. Then something funny happened. Leather Jacket and Pepe became open enemies again.

Pepe, who had never worked for one day in the nineteen years he had been on this planet, called Leather Jacket a phony.

Leather Jacket, still breathing hard, said, "You little uncool Forty-second Street punk."

"Cut it out," I said. But I didn't get up and stop them.

Leather Jacket was ready to attack and ran his trembling hands through his long blond hair.

"You're a real little bitch," he told Pepe. "Did you know that?"

"I'm young, faggot," Pepe cried.

"Oh dear," Coco moaned. "Why do my husbands always turn out to be members of the sisterhood?"

FLASH! A CHICAGO POLL reports that segregation is flowering magnificently in America. Oh my God . . . interesting. Is John Wayne aware of the result of the Chicago poll? Once upon a time, John Wayne let Sammy Davis, Jr., wear that legendary hat in a Rat Pack western. John Wayne has given blacks two roles in films he has directed. One black was perfect for his role: he portrayed a slave. But American blacks are not responsible, according to Wayne. It was not surprising for him to announce in a May *Playboy* interview: "I believe in white supremacy."

Once upon a time, playing cowboy in an old wrecked house, imitating John Wayne, a nail zipped into my lower lip. I still have the memento today. But I want to tell you about Newport Beach, two years ago. Albert Pearl, my friend and tourist guide, pointed his finger in the direction of a palm-shrouded hill and said, "John Wayne lives over there." June Allyson also lives in Newport, I was told time and time again. I remembered her smile, husky intoxicating voice, the childhood MGM movies. But now I am a man; I know what kind of woman June Allyson is. Breathing the dry, clear air of Orange County, I always detected the scent of the far right. The only way I can describe the scent is to say: Inhale ether, or imagine facing a double-barreled shotgun ten feet from where you are presently standing or sitting.

Uncomfortable looking at the sterile, pretty pastel houses, the Sears Roebuck landscaping. All I can think of is golf, insurance, and car agencies. *Reader's Digest,* the Republican Party, and watching Lawrence Welk on a Saturday or Sunday night. In my youth I visited California. I remember San Bernardino, Whittier (Nixon, the future President of the United States, was living there at the time. However, only family and friends were aware of it), Riverside, Pomona. All the streets linking towns. Even then, the place made me slightly uncomfortable. I certainly had never heard of the far right. Joan Didion was a little girl then. Today, the towns remain the same, the people remain the same—the custodians of San Gorgonio Mountain and Death Valley.

No, I do not want to tell you about Newport Beach today. I am in the East, waiting to fly or crack up. And before either happening takes place, let me say: Afroed, slender, Levi bell-bottoms, striped mock turtleneck

shirt, and perhaps a book under my arm, I usually re-
ceive polite, guarded smiles in, say, Merrick, Long
Island, if I ask directions. A visitor, or has one of *them*
moved here?

Afroed, slender, Levi bell-bottoms, striped mock
turtleneck shirt, and perhaps a couple of books under
my arm, I am always the intruder, the rapist, the mug-
ger on—say—Avenue J and Twenty-ninth Street in
Brooklyn. Basically an Orthodox Jewish zone. I respect,
am fascinated by their way of life. But men have landed
on the moon, pollution is the common cold of science.
We're running out of space, and I've been here for four
hundred years, am no longer a stranger. I am only in
their zones to wash dishes. I am underpaid. Almost all
of them would cheat me if they could, and although I
admire their women, it is at a distance. Their women
would have to literally come crawling on their hands
and knees before I would make love to them. But knowing my mood these days, I'd probably laugh, shout an
obscenity, and walk away.

"Forest Hills, Forest Lawn," I joked in the smoker of
a Long Island train. My two white co-workers were
feigning sleep. Already, they had assured me that
things were getting better. I hadn't asked them. The
tone of their voices would make an agnostic quiver with
belief.

The low-income Forest Hills project. The claim of

nonracial motives and the political under-the-table blackjack game—no matter, no matter! The Forest Hills protest is a Forest Lawn monument to American racism. Would the good people of Forest Hills protest if five hundred of their own kind, five hundred of their black counterparts moved in, early one summer morning?

We'll shift scenes here. On the Bowery, the ex-blue-collar workers rage in their drunken or dry leather voices about the mugging blacks, welfare, and what they have done for this country, rage about the lack of police protection. Clean-cut, always with a demitasse of coins, and chain-smoking—their eyes are a seismograph of hate. Is it because of my money, clothes, cigarettes, my deceptive youthful aura, or my blackness? One or all?

Last night I visited an old friend, James Anthony Peoples, who lives just below the frontier of Harlem on Central Park West. We had been out of touch for a long time. Now it was midnight, and the goodies had vanished. There was nothing to do but get a six-pack of beer. I crossed 110th Street and Central Park West and thought: Is it any wonder blacks and whites are walking out on the black Broadway musical *Ain't Supposed to Die a Natural Death*? Eighth Avenue beyond 110th Street is a living death. The rat-infested tenements remain. Neon-lit bars are gripped with fear. Was I the

Man, a new pusher, a new junkie? One bar locked its door because none of the patrons recognized me. There were subway junkies on both sides of the street. Desperation in their eyes, they resembled black ghosts. Dachau survivors. Wearing colorless rags, they were not junkie cool. They were in the caboose of the junkie train. These men and women did not cop and hock stereos, color televisions. Watching their desperate street bits, my heart broke. Life had ended for them. *But not for the people who had created them.*

I finally copped a six-pack in a superette on 115th Street. It was now almost two in the morning. The superette jammed with bobbing, bad-mouthed teen-agers. Vibrancy exploded from them like fireworks. But did they realize that life had already ended for many of them? You can destroy the future's futile dream, your own frustration, your helplessness with drugs, acts of violence.

Stunned, angry, returned to Peoples' apartment and casually asked, "Did Frankenstein's monster kill his master?" Peoples said yes, and I said, Yes, oh my God, yes! What a nice ending for a story.

Bedded at 5 A.M., I woke up much too early. It was now a little after eight of the same morning. A bottle of beer, Scotch, gin, champagne, chartreuse had left no aftereffects. All I wanted or needed was juice, coffee, a cigarette. I stretched erotically on the yellow Danish sofa in the windowless, paneled Bridal Room.

The mirrored reception room reflected countless images of myself, chandeliers, reminiscent of the French Empire. The room fronted a courtyard, roughly 40-by-60 feet; a rock garden in the Japanese manner, while overhead seagulls seem to skate against a lapis-blue sky. I went into the Gold Room. Yummy, yummy: caviar on a bed of melting ice. Caviar, thin little crackers, hard-boiled eggs, and ginger ale would make a great breakfast—which I enjoyed, sitting in a steel chair, glazed like plywood, that I brought in from the school. I breakfasted facing another garden, offering Oriental serenity. But the quiet was broken by low-flying planes.

Where the hell am I?

In the catering section of a temple on Long Island. Last night I and four other "dish" men arrived. A fast, efficient worker, I was asked to stay over. This happens frequently. I go from temple to temple, hoping that my wages will equal my working ability. I would like to take a leave of absence from Jackson china and try writing again. Money and time. Time and money. A dish man spends a lot of time at Madame Sophie's employment agency. And time spent waiting in trains, buses, taxis.

Nevertheless, the following morning, 7 A.M., I was busing across the Williamsburg Bridge, enjoying a splendid red-gold sunrise, headed for a short gig in the flatlands of Brooklyn. Herbie's International restaurant, a pleasant place to work. The pay is always decent. At 8:05, a hungover Harold arrived. It had been a wild party the night before. Harold had had very little sleep. "Chief . . . Charlie," he said. "Some guy made a mess in the men's room."

It started at the door, finger-painted the walls. The enclosed toilet was immaculate. The man's white boxer shorts looked like a psychedelic brown-and-white design and not really revolting—if you didn't inhale or think about it. The fresh-air ceiling fan had been on all night. A sweet, sickening odor lingered in the men's room. I looked at myself in the mirror. It seemed I had been stepping in human excrement for a long time. Bitterness, nausea became my epaulets. I considered America, the majority of people I encountered, dung mannequins wearing masks.

Harold and his wife Lee were unmasked. Harold and I had coffee and apple pie; then I went back to Madame Sophie's. At four that afternoon, ten men for "dish" (two Chinese students from Hong Kong), the race-track-addict chauffeur piled into a station wagon and drove to the celebrated Le Mansion in New Jersey. It's a mother of a place, a bad marriage between Greek Revival and New England colonial. Exquisite banquet rooms accommodate between twenty-five and three thousand people. And, ducks—total confusion. Parties breaking, parties beginning. Guests entering wrong reception rooms. They wore expensive clothes but lacked style. I suppose in their frantic race up the money-and-social ladder, they had forgotten good manners. Waiters, waitresses (the crudity of the waitresses is astonishing, especially a woman who looks like an apple-pie grandmother); the kitchen staff kissed, joked, and drank. "You ruddy-face old bastard. I'm gonna tell my husband!" Other crews arrived, then the young rabbi and *masgiach*.

The hired help ate in the gentile staff kitchen. I had chicken noodle soup and Dr. Brown's root beer, thinking, At least they feed you before the work shift begins —promising.

I don't remember the exact moment when things went bad. Our boss, Mary Louise, a plump vichyssoise black woman appeared, real, motherly. Her second, Uncle Tom's Shadow, was a dapper Dan, harmless. Our dish crew knocked out the previous party's dishes in no time. We were knighted with a cleanup detail in the Belmont Room, which was divided into two parts by a red satin curtain. Tables (set up for a wedding supper) were pushed against the wall of section 1. The reception in section 2 was ending. But most of the guests did not want to leave. "Ladies and gentlemen," the band leader implored, "you are invited to attend the wedding ceremony." The well-dressed guests clamored for hors d'oeuvres, liquor. Waiters, waitresses appeared to be indifferent; they were partying too. A Puerto Rican of African ancestry said, "Everybody lapping up the booze but us. It's gonna be a long night, and I ain't got no grass. We'd better hit the whiskey sours. I know this place. It ain't no ball game."

The whiskey sours gave us courage to tote party paraphernalia up and down four flights of stairs (the service elevator had conked out before we arrived). Le Mansion's staff did not want the dish crew to eat the leftover smorgasbord. They watched us as if we were new floor waxers at Tiffany's. But we foxed them. We'd wheel a beautiful table out into the nineteenth-century incinerator room, rush back for another table like a swift relay team, and feast in the incinerator room, washing down the tidbits with whiskey sours.

By the time we returned to kitchen number 1, bourbon-drinking mother Mary Louise had become Hula Mary. Dyed pale pale blue, carnations haloed her smooth dark hair. She split our dish crew into two groups. Eighteen men, two kitchens. It looked as if everything might run as smooth as a diesel train on a country road. The night dragged on, begat little disasters. Dishwashers disappeared. I questioned Mary.

She offered me petits fours. My polite Hong Kong helper slowly, gingerly, unwrapped the nonbreakable demitasse cups and saucers from Japan. The blasting kitchen radio was also from Japan, like Mary's sterilized rubber gloves.

God has opened the world's greatest stock exchange in Japan, I told myself. But the cut-glass cigarette holders were made in West Germany. The tea was American, Lipton's.

It was now almost midnight. Trying to do the work of three men, I was getting nowhere. Sotted, Uncle Tom's Shadow sauntered in, offering advice. The dish feeder said, "Man. Why don't you go somewhere and fuck yourself?" "Yeah," I added, "we've been working very well without you. Go and have another drink." "I don't know what's wrong with you guys," the sotted Shadow said and departed. A rack of soup bowls hit the red-tiled floor. From kitchen to kitchen to corridor— you could hear a four-letter Mass.

Mother Mary began going through her tough prison-matron bit. Uncle Tom's Shadow returned briefly. We threatened to break trays over his head. Then the kitchen staff began putting pressure on us. Watching the clock, the young rabbi in the gray silk suit wanted to know what was happening. I informed him that his kitchen staff was inefficient and stoned. I even mentioned the Bolshevik revolution, the Black Panthers.

We were getting paid $1.85 an hour. (The majority of caterers paid $2.00 an hour on weekends. Le Mansion had a reputation and even advertised in New York newspapers.) Then, a silence engulfed the kitchen. We continued working until 3 A.M. No overtime. The grumbling kitchen staff took over.

After dressing, we lined up for pay. They took out seventy-five cents for some nonexistent tax. A tip? Tips filter out before the dishwashers have washed the last dish. However, the host and hostess, who usually come into the kitchen after dinner, displaying benevolent smiles, are unaware of the theft.

We waited in the early-morning darkness for our chauffeur to arrive. The sun was up when we arrived in Manhattan.

At home (the Valencia Hotel over-
looking St. Marks Place, conveying a chamber-of-com-
merce aura of decadence, affluence)—I usually avoid
china and glassware. A paper container of iced tea,
laced with brandy, a thin *Post*, a bar-mitzvah cigar.
And *The New York Times*.

MILLIONS IN CITY POVERTY FUNDS LOST BY FRAUD
AND INEFFICIENCY

Knocking ash off my cigar, I sighed and crossed my
legs. Serious too. Like sitting in a comfortable leather
chair at the "club."

Multiple investigations of the city's $122 million-a-
year anti-poverty program are disclosing chronic corruption and administrative chaos . . .

Pouring a straight brandy, I said, "Shit. I could have
told the cocksuckers that two years ago," and continued
to read:

It's so bad that it will take ten years to find out what's really been going on inside the Human Resources Administration, said an unnamed assistant district attorney.

America is still painting a portrait of Van Gogh's "The Potato Eaters." To hell with arts and crafts, H.R.A.! Culture—cunnilingus! Self-serving sodomy! Work projects, lighthearted cleanup campaigns. Music in the streets, dancing in the streets. Perform for the poor. Three mini-vignettes of waste, money, time, inefficiency at a branch of H.R.A. are on the front lawn of my mind.

It's all there. Accounts in Swiss banks. A mysterious George José Mendoza Miller. An elderly man in a cubicle Wall Street office. The pulsating glamour of Las Vegas. Parked cars on a street in Los Angeles (straight out of a television detective series). A $52,000 check with Mary Tyler's private phone number on the back. Now, we'll switch to Amsterdam and it's not tulip time. H.R.A.'s money is so mobile—promiscuous dollars! Now, let's zoom in on the fabulous black "Durham Mob" from North Carolina. Out of sight! A rented car, the fuzz, and Forty-second Street.

Nina, a sensuous black divorcée, mother of three children, has appeared on the front lawn. She has an executive position at an antipoverty agency. Knowing of my financial hangup, she tried to secure a $ gig. I would write reports, Nina would school me. I had autographed copies of *The Messenger* and *The Wig* for her boss and went uptown on a fine, sunny morning.

"The switchboard service is lousy," I said, "and what are all those people doing in the lobby?"

Nina laughed. "Hustling, baby. Everybody wants a piece of Uncle Sam's money."

"But they're well dressed," I protested.

"I know. Only the poor suffer. Same old story."

"Enduring?"

"Yes," Nina agreed, then added: "Bad news, baby. Do you remember meeting a Mr. XX at a party on Riverside Drive?"

"Oh, him. I remember, and his pretentious old lady."

"He said you had a nasty mouth," Nina told me. "Bureaucrats don't like writers. The written word gets them uptight. All they know is numbers, percentages on charts."

"Now if only I was an out-of-work musician. A junkie or a jailbird," I fantasized. "Whitey and niggers dig them."

We laughed, saluted the gig goodbye. Nina sent out for coffee and doughnuts. While we waited, she talked about her program.

"Each time you come up with something that could help the poor, they veto it. I've been warned to cool it at meetings. Like the junkie program and the P.S. 201 thing."

The boy arrived with the coffee and doughnuts. Nina could not wash her lovely hands in the office basin. It had been clogged up for a month. The American government paid a yearly rental of $25,000 for these three old creaky floors. It was not one of Harlem's better buildings.

Nina signed papers, talked on the phone, gave instructions to her secretary. Then she went down in the elevator with me. We talked on the sidewalk and watched the late-summer Harlem scene pass. Nina pressed two tens and a five in my hand.

"Get stoned or laid, baby," she said, then added: "See that sports car on the opposite side of the street? It belongs to an office boy. He's stealing the place blind."

Let's take a trip upstate. The one-way bus fare to South Fallsburg, New York, is almost six dollars. In August 1968, a branch of the Neighborhood Youth Corps spent almost thirty dollars of the government's money sending five young blacks to the Flagler Hotel (Catskill territory). I do not know who paid for their return (I was down at the lake, drinking wine). All I know is that four boys and one girl, well dressed and very clean, arrived one gray afternoon, under the impression that they would become counselors—according to the gospel of the Neighborhood Youth Corps. The boys did not like the living quarters. "Man, it's a barn," I remember one of them saying. But they were young, lived in another world, and did not know that stables, barns are comfortable and sometimes chic.

The girl was signed on as a maid. The boys were to be part of the dish crew. But one boy, a suit-and-tie boy, wanted to work in the office. He said he could type forty-five words per minute. I remember the boy taking his pajamas from his luggage, arranging his shoes at the foot of his bed. I rapped with them in the former stable, then took them to meet the dish crew, who were Southern blacks. Always trying for the diplomat's degree, I tried to open the barrier between them: an impasse. After dinner that night, the hotel manager was perceptive enough to realize the teenagers would not groove in a Catskill scene, and they left the following morning.

Now, you know I am joshing. Is there any wonder why I love fiction? Dig: a friend, Larl Becham, had secured a gig at an antipoverty branch which was preparing a musical for the black community, an end-of-the-season gala. Becham was the choreographer and assistant director. Considering his experience, reputation, the lavish poverty giveaway, he was paid nothing —$100 a week. The teenagers were paid $45 a week to study voice and dance. Most of them were not interested in voice and dance. The boys and girls who were interested in voice and dance were in the Harlem tenements, the streets, sitting on stoops, standing on street corners. The boys and girls I saw at rehearsal had boo-galooed under the wire with connections. I remember one girl, the color of hand-rubbed teakwood. Awkward, sullen, she knocked down $45 a week because one of the "big fish" was trying to make her.

Becham gave me the script to read. Only the author (the director and brother of the agency chief) could relate to the script. It was the type of musical MGM might have considered in 1886 and turned down.

"Can you believe we are opening next week?" Becham asked.

Another brandy, Nathanael West? Let's buy Eartha Kitt Calanthe harrissii orchids, jade, ropes of pearls. Let's listen to her rich, bitter laughter . . .

Before 'Mericans heard of Our Lady of Beautification, Lady Bird Johnson, and before all those black and white performers brought alms to poor blacks, Eartha Kitt, in the late '50's, had her own unpublicized antipoverty program at the Harlem Y.M.C.A. Miss Kitt's first love was dance, and she had been a member of the Katherine Dunham Dance Company. She sponsored the Eartha Kitt Dance foundation. Larl Becham taught the classes. Any black child could take free dance classes. You did not have to be a friend of a friend or have someone get sweaty hands, thinking about how you would be in bed with a couple of drinks, a little pot.

Revolting? I have an idea that one day black and white bureaucrats will succeed in eating Uncle Sam's beard, balls, navel, and the money itself.

Anyway, Birdie Greene, the maid, wants to clean my room, and I have to take the train to Philly, to the City of Brotherly Love.

Shot down in Manhattan, my mood was like F. Scott Fitzgerald's at Princeton. A lost writer in Philly, covering rock's elegant gypsies, Sly & The Family Stone. A taxi strike or what the hell? Popped a couple of pills, encountered the Doubtful Mushroom Company. Waited and waited for the Broad Street bus. Bolted into a Forty-second Street type of zone and found a cab at last.

The Second Quaker Rock Festival was held at the Spectrum Arena. An estimated 8,000-to-10,000 fans had made the pilgrimage. The ritual began at the up-setting hour of 7 P.M. Now, it was 9 P.M. and you couldn't get a beer, babe. The brandy pint was at half mast.

"Too many teenagers," a guard told me. "We don't want no riots out here." Popped another pill, sipped Coke, dug the crowd, promenading in their boutique and department store costumes. They were not as funky and fashionable as the Fillmore East crowd. I expected these earthlings to go home, change clothes, audition for a Crest commercial.

The Creedence Clearwater Revival had finished their set. The Grateful Dead were at the halfway mark, jiving for an audience connection. But the young earthlings were not into it. They prowled around the arena, clowning, taking pictures, searching and copping things such as other earthlings' empty seats. It was like Marat/Sade in Disneyland. They were trying to zap the moment, the night, as if, come morning, they'd be extremely old and wasted. But now, the Grateful Dead was getting next to them with a little theatrics. And suddenly it occurred to me that the swinging '60's will not be remembered for assassins, drugs, pseudo-revolutionary sweat, but for hair and costumes—façades obscuring Andy Hardy interiors and the Girl Next Door.

Between sets, popped the last pill. All those seats like blood ice cubes and red carpeting underneath. An endless collage of cigarette butts. Black faces are rare. There are no young blacks in Philly, I told myself. Perhaps they have gone to the country for the weekend. I counted five interracial couples. "Philly is the northern Atlanta, Georgia," a black told me, adding that a rhythm and blues radio station was now "acid rock" and owned by the University of Pennsylvania.

Another Coke. The Iron Butterfly. A drag, watching

them move in and out with a van of electronic equipment—a space-age cortege. I am not a rock frontiers-
man, as my *Village Voice* readers know. A third-string
convert, my interest goes down like Dow Jones. Now,
Janis Joplin was one of the eight wonders of rock. She
was the only artist capable of making unreality real.
She pressed sincerity against her bosom like a con-
temporary Cleopatra with a humane asp.

Iron Butterfly gave a controlled performance. *Mucho*
things working for them: a light show, fire, the drum-
mer's hypnotic solo. Sly: a tough act to follow. One
fact checked out: whatever followed had better offer
more than peanut-butter-and-jelly sandwiches and
milk. The crowd's mood had changed. Let's-get-this-
show-on-the-road! Little put-down remarks, peachy
hands simulating megaphones. Twisting and turning in
seats like the nursery-school set at a Saturday matinee.
An orgy of fingernail biting. Two-fingered whistles.
The gaiety of floating balloons cooled the action in my
section.

Sly? I had watched the family arrive, single file. I
caught a glimpse of Sly's father, little brother Sidney.
Sly's aide-de-camp, loaded with cameras, directs the
setup. Watching them drag out the electronic equipment, rock fans look bored. Young earthlings go on
unorganized patrols. Then Sly & The Family Stone move
through the semidarkness like secret agents boarding a

ship at dawn. The spotlight doesn't hit Sly until he is at the edge of the revolving stage. Applause is polite. Guarded, as if the waiting, twenty little anticlimaxes had dried the applejack on the fans' hands.

Another delay. A cord, a connection, or some goddamn thing has been misplaced and the Family cannot perform without it. Two earthlings on my right look like the sons of prosperous farmers, but they have a good knowledge of rock. Resting their booted feet on the back of the chair in front of them, one says, "The fucking bastards are gonna take all night. Have you got the keys?"

The lost writer scans the lower arena. Primed with saliva, hoarded energy, they seem to rehearse sons-&-daughters-of-the-Lion's-Club retorts, handed down from generation to generation as the last heirloom in the American attic of—I am white and right and will not be kept waiting! Yes, a hard line separates this mood from that of a hard-drinking black crowd in an East St. Louis dive, or the silence of black balcony girls at the Apollo as blond Chris Connor comes onstage and scats, or the raunchy revolt of the Fillmore East audience. No, this unrest blew from the carved horns of legends, was removed from minds, lips by the second number. Sly & The Family Stone delivered. Through talent, a touch of sorcery, they grabbed the Spectrum fans. They did not have to crack whips, lock exit doors. In the top tiers, earthlings danced. Groovy, man, bravo, swinging; right on became a litany. In the row opposite me, a group of prep-school boys aped wrestling fans. "I hope Sly & The Family Stone makes more money than the other groups," one boy said. A very hip-looking Chinese couple turned around and laughed softly. Three over-thirty couples stood up and ritualistically let it all hang out. But they were dressed like swingers who go to bowling tournaments.

Sly & The Family Stone marched off and around the revolving stage. Hundreds of earthlings rushed to the main floor. Security guards were lost in the shuffle. Incredible. This was rock power, and it had left me exhausted. I did not stay for the last set, Steppenwolf. A good slice of the crowd left with me. It was almost one in the morning and we needed air, fair or foul.

Tuesday before Philly rock night, returned from gigging a fashion-show luncheon. At 4 P.M. the last dish had been washed, and we were paid until 6 P.M. All right! Take me higher, as Sly would say.

But I'm waiting in the lady's pad to get laid; she hasn't showed.

"That is history," said Mae West, pointing toward the Hollywood bed, the headboard, tufted in lime-green plastic.

Hell, "That's history" is *my* line. Sprawled on the blue-tiled floor, higher than a blimp. But together, noting the blind-woman's knitted circle of a rug, folded in the corner like an apple turnover.

I was fingering my worry beads when the lady arrived from Manhattan labors and immediately passed out. She had had too many drinks. Heavy, radical conversation at the Cedar Tavern.

Down, boy. Pop, smoke, and drink.

Meanwhile, the floor had become the Straits of Gibraltar. I could almost hear Moroccan voices. But the voices below the window belonged to illegitimate Boy Scouts breaking whiskey and wine bottle. ¡Olé! Stoned images. The blue-tiled floor, the Mediterranean. Where are the ships at sea? The Algeciras ferry? Molly Bloom has disappeared on Gib. The rock, *a* rock. Fang? Phyllis Diller. A guest shot on tonight's telly? No. The Falangists, celebrating their thirty-fourth anniversary. The Spanish Civil War. Hemingway & company. Communism. The late Joseph McCarthy conducting the last or the first concerto since the Salem witch hunts? A 21-gun salute to that fantastic broad, Miss Virginia Hill. Dorothy Parker, Ayn Rand, James Poe, and the smiling, talkative Elia Kazan. The cold, righteous years. General Eisenhower pirouetting into Korea that winter. We sawed open the wooden floors of our tents and hid the White Horse (white lightning) gin, were forced to march in the rain because our officers were afraid to let us relax in our tents, and our latrine slid down into a ravine when the ground thawed. Hysterical, stoned, bored, frightened, some of us shot holes in the roofs of our tents, tried to shoot bullets at the stars, shot heroin, sniffed cocaine, and went to the whorehouses with the zeal of aspiring politicians. Death had spared us; America was begetting a nation of zombies, or so we thought. "Back home," "back in the world," our countrymen had heads shaped exactly like golf balls. Years passed. I remember a brief moment of splendor and hope. Fail and enter the age of assassination. J.F.K., Malcolm X, R.F.K., Martin Luther King. Men and women protest, march.

They are still marching, according to *The Village Voice*. I'm losing my high and look at the *Voice* photographs: the pseudo-Nazi: upchuck pop art, and below it the chilling, precise portrait of the white-Right, advising: FIGHT THE JEWISH-RED ANARCHY! (Collegiate and apparently serious, the minted middle class are unaware of the Ronald Reagan South African waltz and as upright as backwoods Baptists.)

Next, a group photograph, notable for a girl resembling Susan Sontag. MP's frontlining. Ditto: Black

MP's. An accident, or did the Pentagon believe uniformed blacks could cool the liberal white temper?

Norman Mailer with a part in his hair. Robert Lowell, Sidney Lens, Dwight MacDonald—a group photograph, intellectually heavy. The last photograph: another crowd scene with a banner reading: NEGOTIATE WITH THE NLF.

Smell the hot bacon grease; or are you waiting for it to congeal? Try a side order of cole slaw, dished out to the masses at a box supper. I had roast pork, rice, and beans with the neighbor's nine-year-old son. We clowned over wine and beer, then I chased the barefoot boy out into the street: we ended our cops-and-robbers game. On our block, real bullets ripped the air. The nine-year-old and I witnessed a Saturday-night double murder, a near riot. But by this time, we had become accustomed to the sound of bullets. They seemed unreal, a drag. We raced back into the lady's pad and sipped lukewarm beer.

The next day, Sunday. *The New York Times* arrived (you can never be sure in Brooklyn). Drinking my second cup of tea, I thought about the man with the part in his hair. Norman knows the whole fucking scene, I told myself, looking at his *Voice* photograph again. What the hell is he doing in Washington? Taking the temperature of the Vietnam protest?

Honestly, I can't remember when the Vietnam war

began. My little police action had President Syngman
Rhee of Korea. Drafted, indifferent to the military, I
wanted to emerge from the action, blasé as Hemingway's stepson. Why, protesting, burning draft cards was
unheard of. In my time, regardless of personal beliefs,
young men did their thing. After all, Korea cut the
familial cord. The possibility of war offered escape,
excitement. Death offered a free tour, a trip. Fear cur-
dled our Korea-bound ship. And there were the Dr.
Strangelove inspections. Standing on deck in the cold
and rain. Vomit peppering stairwells, baptizing heads.
But we were very religious and attended Protestant and
Catholic services with the same marvelous indifference.
Old marine Phoenix ship rocked at night, plus Bronx
cheers from crap games, drunkenness, arguments,
fights, nightmares. Hallowed be Thy name and—please
let me sleep.

On the seaborne asylum, most of us tried to stay high.
Fear knighted many of us. Fear was alien to me, and
although I loved the sea—when was I going to see land
and trees? Wading ashore at Pusan, I was grabbed by
something that would not let go. This was not basic
training, bivouac at Missouri's Fort Leonard Wood.
It was a bright autumn morning, and silent, efficient
young soldiers advancing, wading through muddy
water with M-1 rifles held high. Breathless, crawling up
the sandpaper-colored beach. The unreal knowledge of

arriving. Homeward-bound GI's laughingly telling us: "Joe Chink is waiting on your ass." "Buster, you'll be dead before the sun sets."

But there was no fighting, only an uneasy truce. The majority of us were fortunate young men in Korea. We soldiered, worked, screwed, and got high. A nitty-gritty Cinemascope setting, the script courtesy of middle America's veterans from World War II, a script that had to be shot at Universal or Allied Artists. Without realizing it, the GI protégés, we were rehearsing for the '60's.

Ah . . . the moment has arrived. Vietnam, our cancer, or life's booster. A television corn flake commercial, or shall we hum an abstract hymn to the liberal's menopause?

Another angry glance at the *Voice* photographs: Jiveass motherfuckers. Faces I have encountered in person and on the printed page.

A few years ago their kind were marching for the blacks. But nonviolent marching produced sore feet, fear, and the suspicion that one might truly, truly die for the "cause," and, too, perhaps the movement lost its kick, and like those beautiful rich women, who riding sidesaddle creamingly ejaculate, the liberals had quite simply, ladies and gentlemen, found a new cause, fresh with the scent of discovery. A challenge, a map of a situation on which they could embroider *Peace & Love*.

What should the peace-loving earthlings do? Marshal

their forces and elect a President in the forthcoming election who will guide them toward a peace-loving future. That is our only salvation. If they are able to mainline moral reality into the American way of life. If. If. If—

At the moment, mothers, nothing's shaking. From the Pentagon whirligig, right on down to you and you. We are freaking in and out, in and out of the reality around us. But oh, what a marvelous show!

THE GREAT DROUGHT HAS ARRIVED. Dusty pollen falls like snow over Manhattan. Anxiety moans, obscures the sun; the sky seems tinted by a cheap detergent. Listless, suspended days, baked streets. An insane jungle of voices, day and night. *Le malaise* grips St. Marks Place. Earthlings seek not love, drugs, but a strait jacket for the mind, or at least an act of violence to release emotions. A legacy of sundry gifts has been handed down to them: war, pollution, corruption, hate, venereal disease. All of us are involved in the first four bequests. But it seems VD is the province of the young. Ah, Alice! The looking glass has microbes on it—an infected twelve-year-old girl.

You will find VDers in the morning (9 to 11 A.M.) and in the afternoons (1 to 3 P.M.), Mondays and Thursdays (4 to 6 P.M.), entering the public-health centers like members of a secret society. But I want to tell you about the Chelsea Health Center at 303 Ninth Avenue. At one time, I lived near the center. Viewed on a humid afternoon, the Chelsea Center is like a setting for a working-class *The Third Man.* Bureaucratic and faintly sinister. Situated between a public school, a warren of housing projects, and a devastated block that ends at Twelfth Avenue and the Hudson River—this small two-story brick building seems so asexual. One would think that men and women went there to relieve themselves, bathe, or sleep after a sexual quickie or a feast. Yet this small building is the salvation of that dandruff-like disease, gonorrhea.

Mondays and Wednesdays are extremely busy, I was told, plus holiday aftermaths. S.R.O. But first you check in with the receptionist, avoid the children going to the dental clinic, the elderly waiting for X-rays. Male VDers go into a small, crowded waiting room with pale, pale green walls, almost the exact shade of gonorrhea semen. No smoking, please. Bright-colored plastic chairs. Bogart and Marx Brothers posters. Before interrogation and tests, you read, sleep, or watch your fellow travelers. Tense young men who usually acknowledge each other with a sly/shy you-got-it-too grin. The promiscuous earthlings are cool. Conversation between a teenager and his slightly older friend.

"What we gonna do after you get straight?"

"I don't know," the VDer said. "Go to the movies, I guess."

"Are you gonna take Marcia?"

There was no answer. The teenagers were seized with boisterous laughter.

Clapped by the same prostitute, two young mailmen also joked and laughed, crossing and recrossing their legs. An occasional elderly man (looking as if he's on a permanent down), homosexual couples—their faces a portrait of togetherness like expectant parents—are given the nonchalant treatment. But what intrigues me are the young men who arrive with luggage, knapsacks, sleeping and shopping bags. Some of them are from out of town and give false names, addresses, as do Manhattan males. I overheard one longhair give a Washington, D.C., address, complete with apartment number, then ask if a friend could pick up the result of his blood test.

"No," the smiling health aide said.

"Could my sister pick it up? She lives in the city."

"I'm afraid not," the kind, smiling health aide told him, "but check with your doctor."

From my observation, the majority of longhairs are not the supply clerk and other nine-to-five types. Heavy radicals and Marx you I Ching.

I've been down, much too black about the Chelsea Health Center. In the narrow corridor, in the cubicles, occasional funny vignettes.

A male voice (like a recording device announcing time):

"What's wrong?"

"I don't know."

"Take it out."

"Here?"

"Yes" (wearily). Does it hurt . . . burn?"

"Yes, Doctor. It burns like hell."

A conversation in the back room.

"Well. What have we got here?"

The tall blond was silent.

"Jesus! Al, come over here and take a look at this."
The penis inspector and Al made no further comment
about the discovery, except to tell the blond to return
to the waiting room.

Another cubicle conversation.

"Dark field, Miss Norse. Now, young man. Would you
like to lie down or sit up?"

"Sit up."

"I think you'll be more comfortable lying down."

"I'll sit up, I think."

"Very well. Now take it out and turn it toward you."

"Toward me?"

"Turn the head of it toward you."

"Toward me?"

"Yes. Turn the head of it toward you. Sort of swivel
it a little."

Heavy silence during the test. Then: "How long
have you had it?"

"About a week, sir." (An ex-army man in the cube?)

"Does it hurt?"

Deep breathing, confiding tone, "Yes, sir."

"I'm sorry. Dark field, negative. We'll have to do it again."

"Again?"

"Yes," the voice of the doctor drones. "Now take it out so that it faces you. That's good. Hold still. Hold it . . ."

Indeed. Toward you. Indeed. It is in you. Gonorrhea, chancre (the primary stage of syphilis), or advanced syphilis with its nearer-my-God-to-Thee fear.

But the waiting room is bright, congenial. Fear: subtle as dust. After the blood test (stronghearted men break into a cold sweat), the penicillin shot, VDers are in a holiday mood. But—wait. It's not over. The social-worker interview. Everyone gets uptight. You are supposed to be very honest and name names and when and where. But there are the white lies, the loss of memory. Many VDers do not remember who they slept with and give the name of a foe/friend. You will never know the anonymous friend/foe who volunteered your name and address. Fake word-of-mouth also helps spread VD. And, too, it is much easier to detect VD in a man than in a woman. An ancient, misunderstood disease, often hereditary, VD is the thing this year. Our future. Aren't we promiscuous? Swingers in and out of bed? Aren't we top-of-the-morning Americans, seekers of fresh territories, and ever so mobile?

The drift? It continues. Frenzied days and nights. All I want to do is stay stoned; despair is the masochistic lover, chained to my feet as August spends itself slowly; time the miser with the eyedropper. Summer. Summer's end. Will the summer ever end? Will I escape this time?

Returning from another dish gig, I bought the Sunday *New York Times* and read the *Book Review*. You made the news today, boy. But that failed to ax despair. The frustration, the peasant's labor of the night before were still fresh in my mind. After showering, I feel less tense, prime myself with ice-cold beer. It's a mother of an afternoon. The sullen sky gives no promise of relief, rain. The murmurous St. Marks Place voices drift up as if begging for something which escapes them in this elusive city. But booze won't elude me. No. There's half a pint of vodka, and I made a pill connection on St. Marks Place, bought three pints of wine from a "doctor" on the Bowery.

And I sat in my room waiting, watching the sky turn dark, listening to radio rock, inhaling the Coney Island odors that wafted through the window from the nearby pizza parlors, hamburger luncheonettes. The night was a scorcher. Should I hit the streets? Visit air-conditioned friends/foes? Are you jiving, mothergrabber? What could they possibly do except accelerate the drift? So I showered again, opened the door, turned off the bed lamp. The Valencia is an anything-goes hotel.

Finger-popping, dance-marching around the room, wanting desperately to get higher; become incoherent, hallucinate, vomit, pass out. But that never happens. Once again, I was stoned in the hall of mirrors. It's brilliant, beautiful, but fear in the back of the mind bevels the edge. What am I frightened of? Death, aging, my fellow men, madness—frightened that one terrible morning or night I will no longer have the marvelous ability to drink, drink, knock it down, as they say: Yes! Mix it all up, pop a variety of pills, smoke grass and hashish—frightened of what might be my inability to love, although I am loving, generous, understanding with friends, strangers.

Shirley. Memory is a bitch, I think, hitting the cheap white wine. Maggie's latest perfumed note from Paris remains unopened. A difference in age. She had never been able to conceive and I had always wanted a son—

Little Richard rhythmically falsettoing on rock radio. Damnit. Should have married Anna Maria. But it ended badly, since I was having an affair with her sister.

Anna Maria! Stoned, a little uneasy on the first tier of loneliness, self-pity . . .

"Oh, Mr. Wright, are you home?" Birdie Greene, the Valencia maid, asked. "Have you got a cig?"

"Birdie . . . wait till I get my pants or a towel."

"All right."

"Kinda hot tonight."

"Yeah," Birdie said in her Selma Diamond voice. "Damn machine broke again, and I just can't go out in the street. You know what I mean. And those people in 55. Just because they see me, don't mean I'm working."

"Take the whole pack," I said. "I've got more."

"Thanks, Mr. Wright." Birdie Greene smiled. "See you on Wednesday."

Midnight became the world's most uptight jackhammer. Jesus. When would the son of a bitch conk out?

"Hi," the girl said warmly, standing in my doorway. "Have you seen Joe and Helen?"

"Have I seen who?"

"Joe and Helen." The girl giggled. "They live down the hall, and I thought . . ."

"No, baby. I've been looking for Charles Wright."

Blond (why are they always blond?), Levis, pop-art T-shirt, no bra, no shoes, coquette repainting tomboy exterior, clutching a dollar's worth of white-yellow buttoned daisies. (On St. Marks Place with the peace, pot-smoking young, it's a single rose. The deflowered, hip, zipping middle-class Americans, off target, ricocheting—back home.)

"What's happening?" the girl asked.

"What the hell do you think is happening?"

"Wow, man. How you come on."

"Wow, how you come on," I said. "Must all of you say everything that I expect you to say?"

"Aren't the flowers lovely? Peace, flowers, and love, brother."

"Come on in." I smiled and let it pass, flicking on the light. "Let's share a stick of peace."

The girl executed a mock curtsy. In the light I could see her decadent infanta gaze. The infanta, concealing jeweled daggers under the crinolines, a girl-woman with small, hard, cold eyes, fixed on my penis.

"Good grass, man," the girl confided.

"Yeah."

"Your eyes look funny. Glazed."

"A black devil."

The girl giggled again. "No, you're cool, brother. We've got to put the flowers in water or else they'll die."

"Well," I said rising, "we can put some of them in the beer bottle."

"That's cool," the girl exclaimed.

We arranged the daisies in the beer bottle. The girl

bounced on the edge of the bed, keeping time with rock on the radio.

"Do you think you can get me off?"

Silence.

"Come on, cookie. If you want some bread or a place to crash for the night, okay. But don't play. I'm a superb gameplayer. I don't like monkey games."

"Do you think you could love me?" the girl whimpered.

"No," I said, turning off the light. "But let's ball."

The girl, a knowledgeable child, sexually proficient, was kicked out at noon. "Do you love me?" she had asked.

Still high, seeking solitude, yawning, I had turned toward the girl: "What? Get out of here. You're out of your league. A lot of black dudes on St. Marks will buy that jazz. So you'd better get out and find one."

"I've got one," the girl replied bitterly, "and thanks for nothing."

The heat had not diminished, and I went to the corner and bought ice, a half gallon of wine. Returned with my prime minister, *The Drift*. MJQ—the Modern Jazz Quartet was playing on the radio. It was a little after three in the afternoon, and I was knocking down white wine, chain-smoking. Then suddenly I knew what I was frightened of: the daisies in the beer bottle. Goddamn innocents, secretly smiling. Bastards knew I was frightened that something might happen, and I'd never be able to write the book I believed I was capable of writing.

Malcolm, Malcolm. Malcolm Lowry. Has the volcano been sighted?

Anyway, here's a bunch of daisies for the dead dog in the ravine.

AND ON THE FIFTH DAY, I left Manhattan, returned to the Catskills, my seasonal home away from home. I can always go to the Catskills and wash dishes. Real peasant wages, a peasant's caldron. Here —where it's green and serene—these flat, informal, manicured acres. The eye looks upward and sees dense treed mountains, a pearl-blue sky. Tall poplar trees ring the lakes and golf courses. Blacks and Jews may not share a passion for pork, but they do share a passion for Lincoln Continentals and Cadillacs. The Jews seem to prefer air-conditioned cars.

Early afternoon. The pool and cabanas are crowded. A bearded black tyro who will not speak to the black hotel employees plays light George Shearing jazz, which soars in the high wind. Far off, a woman sits alone and knits. Children play volleyball. A well-known Hollywood character actor frolics by the pool. This scene is visible from my window in the former children's dormitory. A pleasant vacation vista. The grind of Manhattan,

Brooklyn, the Bronx is far away. Why move from the lounge chair? The entertainment director is trying to coax people to play games. The guests are indifferent. Perhaps they resent their vacation being regulated by a whistle. "And you're always complaining because there's nothing happening . . . Jesus," the director says into the floor mike.

The indifference flowers. A pleasant young man, a novice politician, makes a brief speech. He has recently returned from Israel. He is not soliciting funds; the young man works out of the Lower East Side, which is a memory (or a business) for the guests. The young man has a fine voice and, to use an old-fashioned, un-fashionable word, is sincere, mentioning briefly the June war. Quotes from the Bible. Warns that peace is a long way off. Israel needs support.

No one is listening, except to their companions; others promenade. The entertainment director is ner-vous. Finally, the young novice politician thanks his apathetic audience, adding that this might not be a proper place to talk but—

By 5:30 that afternoon, most of the guests had left the pool. It had been a lazy afternoon. Israel was far away. The guests would go to their rooms, bathe, rest, and dress for dinner. They had time for an after-dinner walk in the clear mountain air. After all, they gave to the United Jewish Appeal, and they were in the land of the free.

I was free until midnight, moonlighting as lobby porter. No hassle, though. The quiet, secure middle classes have quiet, secure vacations, except for weekends. Occasionally something happens: like the man who had brought a shotgun. It was not the hunting season. Anyway, a houseman stole the shotgun. A kitchen man stole the shotgun from the houseman.

"Fuck the hotel," the kitchen man said. "What has it done for me? I've worked my ass off for nothing. I'm gonna drink wine for a couple of weeks and sleep in the grass."

Up here, wine is king and beggar. A gallon of cheap wine can destroy a $5,000 bar mitzvah. The hotel owners are aware of this—and, well. But it is profitable to them, regardless, if crisis follows crisis.

Witness: the pot-and-pan man was alone and extremely well for five days. After a fifth of must-I-tell (muscatel) wine, he's packed his California suitcase (a California suitcase is a brown paper bag, cardboard box, or shopping bag) and announces that he is quitting. Pissed because he had to wash walls, a dishwasher decides to quit also. The head dishwasher is on a drug safari.

A pantry man decides to hit the road with his buddies. Last night, the nightclub porter pissed in the sink and got fired. Two housemen went into town and never returned. Another has been stoned in the dormitory for two days. The salad man swaggers in with a fifth of Scotch and is escorted out of the kitchen. A middle-aged kitchen man, a professional, chases the smart-aleck second cook with a meat cleaver. The baker, a former marine, is stoned as usual. Between offering bear hugs, he throws wads of dough. A day behind the scenes in a Catskill hotel; you take it as long as you have to, or split. The working and living conditions are terrible. No unions or overtime, which is why hotels fail to secure stable employees. You work long enough to get wine money or "talking back" money and move on. But— Monticello, the mountain Las Vegas, beckons; the police wait; and it is ten and ten: a ten-dollar fine or ten days in jail, or both. Now you are no longer required to see a judge, go to jail. You give the policemen ten dollars, and he drives you to another hotel, regardless of whether or not you want to work. Labor Day is near; the hotels are desperate. This year, the Bowery men are not making their annual Catskill expedition. A man might as well panhandle, eat at the Municipal Lodging House on East Third Street, and sleep in a doorway. Why should they work twelve hours and get paid for seven? And may I wish the Bowery men a happy holiday.

At this particular hotel, the only happy people are the guests and the young black men from Alabama who will work the summer season and hope to return home with $500 or $300. Like the Puerto Ricans, they work hard, save their money, and stick together. A natural-born citizen of the world's most prosperous country, I tremble to think of what life back home is like. But that's another story. A chapter of the story is in the beautiful, legendary Catskill Mountains, in the great and small hotels, bungalow colonies, where once Jewish workers came to relax from Manhattan sweat shops, gangsters came to play and kill. Now, small towns and cities bear ancient Indian names, and progress and builders have raped the wilderness, and money, anxiety, anger, greed dance through the clean mountain air like a chariot filled with lovers.

Indifferent, unchanging world—that's it in the final analysis, I remember thinking one night. There was a full moon. With coffee and cigarettes for company, I went down to the lake. I thought of F. Scott Fitzgerald's Dr. Dick Diver. Yes. Tender is the night. I became frightened and left the following morning.

Back home. Back in the summertime city, laying sevens against the nitty-gritty. Manhattan and the good life. The pace, the anonymity. A challenging, wondrous city. But do I want to stay here? In fact, do I want to stay in the United States of America? I have never felt at home here. Ah, memories of the old days! Obscured by green cornfields, I wanted to play seek and ye shall find. But the mothergrabbers felt more like a crude game of croquet; their mallets tried to split open my head with a golden eagle's beak. Pressing Onward in 1972, I fail to dip into that fondue of phrases, Right On, Brother or Right On, America, although the masses are ever so Aware and Hip, blessed with the technical realities of the space age. I've got dt's in the rectum. "This world ain't my home," grandfather used to say. Ah yes! I'm coming from the edge of despair. Booze and pills fail to ax despair. I always get stoned on that frightening, cold level where everything is crystal clear. It's like looking at yourself too closely in a magnifying mirror.

Weighed down with my medals of merit from Catskill labors, a wailing Lourdes platoon tap-dancing in the center of my brain, I checked into the Valencia Hotel.

The pale blue room was immaculate. Surprise! No cockroach welcome. The parquet-patterned linoleum gleamed. But the floor was slightly uneven, and the linoleum squeaked like a man snoring. After showering, poured a stiff vodka, moved a straight-back chair over to the window. In the middle of the afternoon, you could

174

feel the heat rising around the sad, stunted trees of Third Avenue, dwarfed by the soot-caked, red-brick façade of Cooper Union. Traffic was a daisy chain of giant drunken crickets. Dressed in colorful summer finery, the teeming crowd, shuttling east and west, seemed exhausted, as if they were being manipulated by sadistic puppet masters. Was the pollution count unhealthy?

"Fair weather, fair weather," I said aloud, and began to doze.

What time was it? Where was I? In a post-sleeping-pill daze, the room was familiar. But I took another shower and recovered. It was five in the morning—that blessed hour. The streets were deserted, and with my quart of vodka, I walked under a starless, subtle electric-blue sky to the Chinese Garden. A solitary man slept on a cardboard mattress; half a loaf of Wonder Bread lay at his feet. The new lane of the Manhattan Bridge hadn't opened. Through the line of trees, I saw a squad car park on the lane. Two exhausted or goldbricking policemen sacked out. An old story. I had been coming here for a very long time.

I began knocking down drinks. When I looked up, a tall woman was coming toward me, moving with a slow, back-country woman's stride. Close-cropped gray hair, print cotton dress, and red-leather house shoes. She was like a curio, a ghost from Hell's Kitchen, a bit player from a Clifford Odets revival.

"Has a man passed through here?" the woman asked, her voice hoarse, hesitant, like a record played at the wrong speed.

"No. I've been here about an hour. I haven't seen anyone."

"I wonder where he went to. Some colored fellow has been following me all up and down the Bowery."

Jesus. One of *them*. Gritting my teeth, curling my toenails, I smilingly said, "Is that so?"

The tall woman nodded. She did not look at me. My vodka held her interest. "That's right. He just kept on following me and saying things. Every once in a while, he'd do something dirty."

"That's terrible. Why didn't you call the police?"

"What good are they?"

Chuckling, I offered the woman a drink.

She read the vodka label carefully. "This ain't wine."

"No," I sighed, "but it gets to you. One hundred proof."

When the woman finally released the bottle, she was panting. "Too strong. Wine's all right. Just like drinking soda pop, and you can get drunk, too."

"Cigarette?"

"You think I'll kiss it. But I won't."

"What?"

"You've got your goddamn hands between your legs."

"I've also got a cigarette in my hand. I have no intention of burning Junior."

"You can't make me do it," the tall woman said.

"Lady, have another drink and beat it. I'm getting a peaceful high, and I don't want you to zonk it."

Frowning, the woman reached for the vodka. "I won't do it. You Spanish and colored men are always following me, trying to make me do things."

"Well," I began slowly, "I am a man of color, but there isn't a goddamn thing you can do for me." The woman shuddered. "Have I made myself clear, bitch?"

"I'll have another cigarette, then I'll go," she said quietly.

Now it was light, but the sun was still behind the tenements on the Lower East Side. It was a lovely dawn, quiet and cool. Early Saturday morning, and there was almost no traffic on the bridge. A few trucks going to and from Manhattan.

I forgot about the woman until she said, "That wasn't a nice way to talk to me."

"And it wasn't very nice of you to disturb me. Do I have to wear a goddamn sign that says I want to be alone?" I jumped down from the ledge and lunged at the woman. "Move, bitch!"

"All right," the woman said, starting off. "I ain't gonna ask you for another drink."

"Goodbye."

"I never said I wouldn't kiss it."

"Get out of here," I shouted.

The woman turned, hesitated, then came toward me. "Can I have another cigarette? That'll hold me till the bars open. That's all I want. One or two cigarettes. I ain't begging. You can't make me do it for no cheap-ass drink."

"Lady, take a couple of cigarettes and make it. I want to be alone. Can't you fucks understand that?"

The woman looked up at me with a hard, angry gaze and accepted four cigarettes. "You're a smart aleck. Well, I don't have to be bothered with your kind."

"You wanna kiss it?" I joked.

"You can't make me do it."

"Hell. Doesn't anyone fuck any more?"

"Rotten bastard."

"Come here," I said.

"Oh, no, you don't," the woman screamed.

Forcing a Great Depression smile, I grabbed the woman's arm.

"You can't make me do it."

The woman didn't try to break from my grasp. I released my hold. "Well, mama?"

The tall woman with the back-country stride did not

move. I looked at her tired, middle-aged face, reddened from wine, the cold gray eyes, watery like tarnished silver. It would have been impossible to kiss the thin, pale lips, and her chest was almost as flat as mine. The idea of dogging this woman, who was descended from thin-skinned rednecks, didn't appeal to me. Unlike many American black men—I have never had a super-charged, hard-on for white women. All I saw was a masochistic woman who wanted to serve Head.

Laughing playfully, I forced the woman's head downward to get a reaction.

The tall woman kissed the head of my penis deli-cately once, the second time with feeling. She went down with the obedient movements of a child. She was a passable Head server. I wanted her door of life and pushed her down into the grass.

"You can't make me do it," the woman cried. "I don't know what you think I am."

"Shut up."

"Rotten bastard."

I stood up and couldn't control my laughter. "Get out of here."

"I wasn't bothering you, and I never said I wouldn't kiss it," the woman cried. "Could I have another drink?"

Aɴᴏᴛʜᴇʀ ʟᴀᴛᴇ sᴜᴍᴍᴇʀ's ᴍᴏʀɴɪɴɢ with the humidity holding tight, no chance of rain. Angry traffic jammed. Silently people trot forward as if they were Communists. But I'm moving, moving fast, checking into the Kenton Hotel on the Bowery. I must stay skulled and get my head together, guard the mini-bank account. I must hold on, hold on, and wait for summer's end. Will the summer never end? The Kenton's mare's nest is cheap, fairly clean (this was before the junkie takeover, before the W.P.A. Off Broadway project moved next door). The hotel proper is on the second landing. You walk up steep marble steps, ancient, Baltimore-clean. You imagine that a Jim Dandy tripped up these steps after having a few with Eugene O'Neill's Iceman. But that was a long time ago. After high noon, you will be accosted by muggers, drunks, panhandlers. Those clean, cracked marble steps will be inhabited by sleeping, wounded, or dead men. You will inhale excrement, urine, vomit. Nausea builds; blast-off time is seconds away; and you are blinded by the bone-white brilliance of the steps and walls; and you have a sense of falling and become frightened. Where are you going? What are you doing here? What happened? "My God!" the self-pitying other voice cries. No matter, no matter.

So you grit your teeth, breathe carefully, take one step at a time. Ah! There is the great varnished door, the glass upper half a mosaic of fingerprints—but you've made it. Safe.

Skulled in the whitewashed cubicle, where the ceiling is high like in an old-fashioned mansion. Chicken-coop wire encloses the top of the cubicle. But there is no air. Only pine disinfectant, roach killer. Countless radios, two phonographs, and one television blast—this is the upper-class section of the hotel, and all the transient men are black.

The bed is lumpy with thin gray sheets, uncomfortable, like a bunk on a troop ship. No matter, no matter. There is a jug of mighty fine wine, a carton of cigarettes. I dismissed the voices, the music, the odors. I checked in to get my head together and write, but a few soldiers from the Army of Depression broke ranks. Now they brought up the rear. When would the bastards make it back to company headquarters?

Stoned, feeling surprisingly good, walking down Broadway, below Fourteenth Street. Less than a block away, I spot this dude on the opposite side of the street. There's something about his movements. Something isn't kosher, I'm thinking, as the dude crosses over to my side of the street and eases into a dark store entrance. It so happens this is where I turn the corner. Now, we're on the same side of the street. But he's in the store entrance of his corner, which faces Broadway, and I'm turning my corner, going west, picking up a little speed.

And who comes cruising along but "Carmencita in blue." Just tooling along like two men who are out for a good day's hunt in the country.

The squad car pulls over to the curb, and I go to meet them. The driver seems friendly. He's smiling. "Do you have any ID?"

"No. Some son of a bitch stole my passport, and I wish you'd find the schmuck."

"Where do you live?"

"Down the street. I'm sure I can find something that will verify who I am."

A brief silence. Calm as an opium head, I casually lean against the squad car.

"Are you the good guys or the bad guys? You see, I'm out to save the city from corruption like you guys. I'm working on my sainthood this year."

The cop sitting next to the driver takes off his cap and runs his hand through his straight, dark hair, which is combed back from his forehead. His nose is shaped exactly like a hawk's.

"He's too much," Hawk Nose said.

"Jesus," I lamented. "Are you guys stoned or am I stoned?"

The pleasant driver liked that one. He was getting his jollies off, and so was Charles Wright.

Then Hawk Nose came on with: "We're looking for somebody. We wanna bust somebody's balls."

There was a touch of cold reality in his voice.

Equally real, I replied, "Well, if you bust my balls, you'd better leave me on the sidewalk."

Still smiling, the driver made a playful lunge for his gun, or what I hoped was a playful lunge.

Hawk Nose, still in his tough, cop-shitting bag, was visibly irritated.

"There was a robbery a few minutes ago," he said,

"and you fit the description of the guy. Height, weight, everything."

Everything meant color. And for a second I had a high fantasy of someone trying to masquerade as me. I started to tell them about the dude in the store entrance. But he didn't look like me and had probably disappeared anyway.

So I stood up straight and waited for the next line.

It was a long time coming; no doubt they were turning different endings over in their minds.

"You'd better not do anything," Hawk Nose warned, "or else we'll lock your ass up."

"Good morning," I said, smiling.

And two of New York's finest rode off into the lambent dawn.

The homosexual has come of age, displaying what he has always hidden, mentally, physically—testicles. Yet despite Gay Lib, there are enough unregistered closet cases to form a commonwealth about the size of Puerto Rico. But the types I'm concerned with here do not belong to either world, yet are as united as grass to earth. That third army of men. Buddies. Masturbating movie-goers, traditional shirt-and-tie men, images of father and grandfather. The ruddy-faced retired firemen, with the *Daily News* turned to the racing results. But hot lips wants to race down. Men who go to cheap movies and bars where three drinks will cost the price of one. Not much has been written about the Homosexual Bowery, where masculine sex outnumbers "girlie" sex.

In moments of grand depression, I think of myself as the Cholly Knickerbocker of the Bowery, writing about young and old men in the last act of life. Men who sit in the foyer of hell as they wait to be escorted into the ballroom of death. But it is always cocktail hour for the "girls" who are sometimes called garbage and ash-can queens. Their past lives and wine have pushed them beyond *The Boys in the Band.* I'm thinking of one queen in particular. Now what kind of female would wear a ratty fur jacket on a summer morning? But once he/she sort of had it together: white-framed dark glasses, jet-black dimestore wig, white halter, lime-green shorts (before the hot-pants vogue), plus a wad of dirty rags. This queen not only wipes off car windows at Houston and Second Avenue, but tries to engage motorists in conversation and, like a visiting celebrity, hops up on the hood of a car, announces: "I've just arrived from Hollywood." You may laugh or choke with disgust but the queen is for real. Sometimes 5 P.M. traffic is stalled: the queen is dancing, waving to her fans.

The closet cases are another story. Masculine, they

open under the toll of whiskey and wine. Masculine gestures give. A grand lady is talking, inviting, and to hell with the buddies, the bartender, the crowd of regulars. No matter, no matter, the closet is open. Until tomorrow. But we've been to that country before, too, haven't we? At least we have read the travel folders, and our friends have visited that country. Well, now we're heading down the trail, deep into Marlboro country (before the appearance of James Jones's *From Here to Eternity* Pall Mall cigarettes were considered effete. Now Pall Mall is the "hard-hat" cigarette, the jail-house cigarette). The Marlboro men would be the first to admit it, sober or stoned. These men have been the backbone of our army, navy, and marine corps. Many of them were the heads of families. Most of them blame the opposite sex for their defeat. So they turned to whiskey, wine, and the company of men.

They do not hate women. They avidly watch and comment on the hippie girls and the blue-collar Puerto Rican and Italian women of the neighborhood. On payday and welfare day, most of them never get laid. But a surprising number of them have each other. Between the "weeds" (any place where the grass is high), jail, and prison, and the for-men-only hotels of the Bowery . . . something happened. Who lit the first flame and where? All I know is what I'm going to tell you.

In most cases, I do not even know their names. But

I have seen them on the Bowery for a long time and have kept a mental file on them. I know the clean-shaven ex-army sergeant will be on the sidewalk come morning. About a month from now, he will look as he does this morning. I know the pipe-smoking old sailor has a photographic collection of nude teen-age boys.

I know that at high noon, two winos entered the Chinese Garden. Each had a pint of La Boheme white port. They sat on the second entrance steps and talked and drank as men will do. Then one of them sprawled out, resting his head on the other's leg. He's passing out, I thought. But his friend looked down at him and caressed his face. The man turned his head and went down. At high noon. In full view of passing traffic.

The father and son are a Bowery legend.

"Oh, shut up," said the queenly father in a tough voice.

"Listen," the son told him. "I went out and worked to buy that wine. Don't tell me to shut up."

"Snotty-nosed bitch," the father said.

"You're just mad because I love John Wayne."

Now in my time I have observed quite a few men and women serving head. But the first prize has to go to a crew-cut man in his early thirties. There is a solid, Midwestern look about him. Even now he looks as if he owns a small successful business and can afford to take his family to New York for a holiday. If he is not self-employed, he is his boss's backbone. I suppose that is why he serves head with such passion. The other day, Crew Cut was going through a desperate scene in the Chinese Garden. His trick was a nervous little man who kept scanning the garden, while folding and unfolding a newspaper. He looked at me, crossed his legs, and pretended to read. It was very comical. I felt like saying: "Get with it and don't mind me. I am communing with my thirty-nine trees." Finally, Nervous Joe tried to block my view with the newspaper.

On another occasion, just before darkness set in, a young white man and a slightly older, slender black man were sitting about twenty feet from me, drinking dark port wine. They were sitting near the street light. But did I really see the black man place his head between the other man's legs? No, my eyes are tired, my mind is tired.

Presently the two men got up and walked over and sat down under a tree, almost directly in front of me, the sidewalk separating us. But I could not hear what they were saying. All I could do was watch the black man stretch out on the grass, then turn to the young white man, who sat with his back against the tree. Finally, he stood up, and I heard him say, "I'll see you around."

The slightly older black man decided to pay me a visit.

"What's happening?"

"Nothing," I said. "I don't have a goddamn thing."

"Wish I could help you."

"But you can't," I told the man.

He thought about this briefly, then spotted a tall, longhaired blond man walking through the garden. He took leave of me and ran after the tall young man, who ignored him. Nevertheless, the black continued to run down his game. He puts his arms around the blond man. Suddenly the blond swung at him, and one, two, three, the fight was on. The blond had the slender man pinned against a tree and cursed him. The slender black man rubbed the blond's buttocks. The blond bolted up from the ground and walked away silently with the black following. They stopped and began talking. The slender black man tipped up on his toes and kissed the blond's lips. The blond young man protested but relented, and then they moved over into the tall grass and made love.

And why are they more comfortable talking about baseball than about their sex lives?

Mail arrives as if programmed by a doomsday computer: P.E.N. dues, Xeroxed McGovern letters, Museum of Modern Art announcements and bills, a request to subscribe to a new *little* magazine for twelve dollars per year; they would also like me to write for them, gratis. Another one of Maggie's HELP notes from Paris.

Dear Charles:

What the hell is going on? Are you all right? You haven't invited me to the States. In fact, you said nothing. Should I return to the States? Well, the goddamn French are out of town. A holiday and I am grateful. Received a goddamn letter from my brother. He's a square-headed, cheap son of a bitch. I tore up the letter and went out and got stoned. But the following day, I received a wonderful letter from Mother. I don't know how she does it. She's in a wheelchair now but still advises the garden club, plays a mean game of bridge, etc. I felt rather good after Mother's letter. But I've got to get out of Paris. I've had the goddamn French. I was thinking about Spain. Shit. I'd probably run into M., the bastard. He still owes me a bundle. I heard he was on Gib, gambling. Mister Big-Time Spender. Why don't we meet somewhere? Do you have any money? Is the book finished yet? I will have to sort of tuck in until the first of the year which means no new clothes.

But if I were back in the States, I could shop at Klein's, Orbach's. Take care and write. WRITE. Remember: I am your friend.

Love

Maggie

Visited my broker, who has an office at First Street and the Bowery. Tony is familiar with junkies, artists, and writers. He remembers Kate Millett from the old days. I pick up the portable typewriter, chat briefly with Tony, and make it up to the Kenton.

"I am a writer if I never write another line," Tess Schlesinger wrote many years ago. No doubt it was a euphoric moment. But I've lost that passion. Scott Fitzgerald and his dazzling green light! His rich, hopeless dream: "Tomorrow we will run faster, stretch out our arms farther."

But I'm knocking down wine, have swallowed my sixth Dexie of the day. A goddamn tic has started under my right eye. I have almost a dozen books that I've read and enjoyed. Then read, son of a bitch.

I stare at the typewriter, mounted on a gray metal nightstand, have a great fantasy: Miss Carolyn Kizer has jumped off the Washington Monument. Miss Kizer did not respond to my request for an application from the National Council on the Arts. Even after I got important people to intercede for me, it was another month before the lady replied. Ah! She was sorry to hear of my financial difficulties. The lady had recently read marvelous reviews of my bête-noire novel *The*

Wig. The novel had been published almost four years ago, and government funds were tight, but would I be interested in a job as writer-in-residence at a small black college in the South?

Absurd truths, absurd lies. Drinking again and re-membering when—the United States Information Agency used certain passages from *The Messenger*. And one heard and read of writers who had received grants and hadn't published one book, or writers who had received grants and were reviewed on the back pages of the Sunday *New York Times Book Review*. One also heard of writers who received grants because they knew someone or had slept with someone.

Perhaps I should follow the advice that I've been given over the years: buy a tweed suit or whatever type of suit is fashionable at the moment and make the literary-cocktail *la ronde*. You know, even blacks do it.

And your father or my father might do it. I'll never do it: But I'll knock down more wine and go out on the fifth-floor fire escape of the Kenton Hotel.

From this distance the view is glorious. The pollution screen even filters the burning afternoon sun. There is no breeze. A sort of suspended quiet, although I can see traffic moving down Chrystie Street; children playing ball in the park; drunks in twos and threes, supporting buddies like wounded soldiers after the battle of defeat. Toward the east, a row of decayed buildings has the decadent beauty of Roman ruins. But only at a distance. Trained pigeons, chickens, and junkies inhabit those rooftops. Taking another drink, I think: I wish I could fly, fly, far away.

Here, there, again, and always, the Why of the last seven years. Skulled depression as I sit and watch the sun disappear. Aware of the muted, miscellaneous noises that drift up from the street, I am also aware of the loss of something. Thinking of all I've done and not done. Thinking and feeling a terrible loss.

"Man, they jumps," Sam exclaimed. "Didn't you know that?"

Sweet-potato brown, Sam has a Hitler, Jr., mustache. An ice-pick scar outlines his left cheek like a nervous question mark. His small bright black eyes seem to recede as if the sight of another pair of eyes was somehow indecent. We had worked together briefly in the Catskills, and I had helped him through several bad Manhattan scenes. His wife had taken the three children and gone to California with another woman. Sam's running buddy, "Two-Five," a thirty-three-year-old crippled Vietnam veteran, was beaten to death on the Bowery. But Sam was laid back now. He had it together. A wide-brimmed, eggshell, plantation straw hat raffishly knocked back on his head. The thin white body shirt was new. He wore lilac bell-bottoms, trimmed in red. The Florsheim patent-leather boots had a permanent shine.

"You can't even see the motherfuckers," Sam said.

"I thought you said you could."

"You can't see the babies, and even the big ones are like spies. They good at hiding out."

"Oh shit, baby."

"Wait until they start walking." Sam laughed.

"Man, are you putting me on?"

"It ain't Mission Impossible. Now, do like I told you. I'll check with you later. Gotta go to Brooklyn and see my sister. She's fighting with the landlord again."

Frequently, on the Bowery, I had seen dirty winos enter and wipe off chair seats with their hands. I always marveled at this small gesture: there was still a touch of human pride in the men. In my novel *The Wig*, Mr. Sunflower Ashley-Smithe says, "I keep a dozen milk bottles filled with lice so I won't be lonely." I had slept around through the years, but I had never encountered lice. Small wingless insects, parasitic on men, especially Bowery men, and the sons and daughters of the Flower Generation.

They were in my hair, under my arms, in the jungle of pubic hair. I itched and scratched day and night. You could take the large ones in your hands and crush them; they made a crackling sound, their blood was crimson. But the poor babies were interesting. Imagine a dozen white angora kittens about the size of pinheads, taking their first steps, crawling against the collar of your brand-new black knit shirt. Genocide, baby. Burn the shirt, shower, shower, shower. I anointed my body with so much oil that I was under the delusion that I was the Sun King, reincarnated.

Toward 6 P.M. after the tic under my eye was sated and I could no longer stand the bone-white cubicle, after I had controlled my impulse to throw the typewriter out the window, I popped another Dexie, desecrated the wine bottle, and later joined the residents in the lobby to watch the news. This was the garrulous hour. Some of the men had returned from work, others from panhandling and dinner at the Municipal Lodging House around the corner. This was the hour of camaraderie, con games, great lies, illegal drinking, loneliness, anxiety.

Always skulled, I made my way through the crowd, exchanging brief, social greetings. Then, sat on the windowsill, trying to concentrate on the six o'clock news or staring out the window.

Against the deep blue of early evening, they turned

on the spotlight at the Holy Name Mission and church at Mott and Bleecker Streets and you could see the white-and-gold-draped statue of Jesus Christ. It was not a life-size statue. From a distance, with the lights playing on it, Jesus Christ was larger than life. Sometimes He appeared to move. Extend His hand, turn slightly. Desperate, I needed a lift. Take me higher. Ground the motors of the stock cars racing in my brain. But "God never worked very well with me," Hemingway's Lady Brett Ashley said. Somehow I can't get in step with the masses and their current religious phenomenon, seeking belladonna for the soul. Tricky business, too. For what is religion but the act of levitation?

It would be much better if I read Malcolm Lowry's *Under the Volcano.* Through his despair, I might be able to understand my despair, to cut the loss, elevate hope.

Of course, I was unable to do this. I did not even reread *Under the Volcano.*

The blank space is self-explanatory. There were a series of days and nights that I do not want to remember. Someday. Perhaps.

I lost love because the threat of insanity, suicide, and murder began to tango around the perimeter of that love.

Someone stole my passport.

I sold the typewriter, radio, and books.

I lost my grandmother's wedding band.

I kept my blackness.

I always felt like a refugee among foe/friends, friend/foes.

I lost my head at last. I watched my head boogaloo happily down the street. As Head desires.

However, one irrefutable truth remained: I could always return to the Catskills.

THIS CATSKILL SCENE is a Japanese water color: white poplar and pine-trees command the fields; the mountains are shrouded in green. Serenity becomes a silent song. Then, suddenly, the sun is smothered by gray clouds. It's an Idaho sky, a pensive Hemingway sky, and you know you are in America. The eye travels out across the land: a buff-colored, shingled ranch house in a clearing of young trees. Fronting the house like emblems are two late-model cars, which spell money. Closer at hand, beer cans litter the wild grass like baubles from the moon. About a dozen butterball kittens are playing in the grass. Running, leaping, rigid before the moment of attack, their multicoloring becomes a shifting pattern in this unofficial season of death.

Originally this was hunting country. It still is, in a restricted sense, although No Hunting signs are everywhere. Vodka-mellow, I like to believe that Hemingway would have felt at home up here— Here where in summer young deer frolic like schizoid ballet dancers. But I wonder what Papa would think about the cats. "Any time you decide to shoot cats, it's the cat season," a man said yesterday. However, no one has said that it is the perfect season to hunt and harass men. Let me ease your mind: that, too, fuses in the clear air like the simultaneous orgasms of lovers.

The lower-echelon employees do not talk of love. It's always other hotels, booze, the Bowery, weapons. None of them own weapons as far as I know (should I write regretfully or gratefully?). Most of them are small-town men, accustomed to the hunting seasons and to being hunted in the ghettos of our towns and cities. Now all they have is this transient gig for a day, a week, a month. Loneliness is a mothergrabber for them.

I would not like to look into their eyes without the cats. In the evening, the cats silently sit on the porch of the kitchen-help house and wait for dinner. Sometimes the men steal tuna fish and tinned milk for their favorites. I am neither lonely nor a fanatical cat lover, but I buy cartons of milk for them. I find myself talking to them in the evening. Questioning them about their lineage, calling them every mother in the book, carefully pouring milk into the tuna tins.

Several ingenious men have built cat shelters out of

cardboard boxes and remnants of carpeting. Some of them are violently jealous of the new kittens in the underground staff dining room—where at this very moment an argument has begun—and ends abruptly as one of the contestants exits with: "Fuck you. I'll see you in Monticello." A weekend employee turns toward me. He is eating Sacher cake and says, "Somebody is gonna break that son of a bitch's neck." This small man, who is very fond of sweets, is my dinner conversationalist, although we rarely sit at the same table.

Nodding, the small man smiles. "Yeah. Last week I bought a rifle for self-protection. Yeah. Up here you gotta be nice or they'll get you."

My dinner conversationalist is unaware of what I am writing and continues to rap, the Sherlock Holmes cap obscuring his eyebrows. A man's skull was fractured on the stone floor beneath my feet. A dishwasher was knifed to death two miles from here. And they never found out who killed the maid in——. Two motorcyclists killed a man, dumped his body in the waterfall, which is a fifteen-minute walk down the hill.

I question my friend about cats. "Yeah. They all right," he says. "I got two in Monticello. They nice."

Cats—common domestic mammals kept by man as pets or to catch rats and mice. Sometimes roasted over an open fire or the base of a succulent stew at Starvation Hour. But for the moment, the United States of America is the richest country in the world. We do not have to worry about domestic cat on the menu—or do we?

Certainly, I wasn't thinking about cats when I went to visit Joey. In the sunflower brightness of a Thursday afternoon, I walked four miles to Joey's hotel, stopping off at a roadside café for a cold six-pack.

Joey offered vodka at ten in the morning. Why not, as we used to say in Tangier. We began drinking and exchanging local news. Then, shortly before twelve, the sound of bullets interrupted our conversation.

"Whenever a hotel has too many cats," Joey, an old Catskill hand, explained, "they shoot them." At lunch Joey pointed out the two men who had killed the cats. The "second," a transient mental-hospital patient, was Mr. Clean. His head was shaped and glowed like a choice eggplant. The main man was lean and rather placid. I watched as he placed his elbows on the white trestle table and hand-rolled a perfect cigarette. The second scooped up the dead cats with a shovel and threw them down the hill. Joey remembered a record by the DC-5 titled "Bits and Pieces."

Postscript: Exactly one week later, at my home away from home, the local fascisti shot more unwanted cats at dusk. House cats and favorites survived.

On my dishwasher's day off, I walked four miles into the village of Monticello, shopped around, paid my respects to several bars, and returned to my kosher hotel. I hoped to spend a quiet day reading, finding out what was going on in the world. But it was payday. The transient workers were doing their thing, celebrating their past and future, the low cost of labor. I drank with them. Skulled in the middle region of my mind, returned to my room, and began reading *Time* magazine. The black print kept slipping off the slick white page. Sleep came down like a knockout drop.

Morning arrived gray and disfigured. The afternoon was a merciless drag. Skulled again, I watched reality enter the kitchen. The bearded Puerto Rican "captain" (the dining-room porter) sat down on the floor and removed his shoes. A melodrama would end if someone moved a stack of plates twelve inches. Tottering old drunks put iced-tea glasses in the wrong plastic rack. A young black takes exactly twenty minutes to put on his apron. Fat Boy tells the fourth version of the woman he did not have on his day off.

On the lunch break, the dishwasher went to his room and tried to sleep. His mind double-timed. Perhaps he would stay in the Catskills forever. Too much, too much, I thought, while the building rocked with the beat of an army payday. I felt as if I had been riding a headless horse for a long time, and kept turning on the mattress. My penis rose as if to protest against the virginal fast. "You should masturbate," I said in a marzipan voice. Why was I always so sexually alert in the country, where the score was zero? New York City was impotent. Cold, corruption, hate had corroded the last vault of reality. Then I remembered *Time* magazine. It was quite by accident that I flipped to page 81—The Press. A magnificent photograph of Norman Mailer centered on the page. A tough, intelligent face outlined with compassion. The face of an urbane carpenter in a $200 suit. This emotion was enlarged by the dishwasher's respect for the man. They had met several times and had exchanged notes through the years. Certainly Mailer was the best writer in America. He was one of the few writers who could force the dishwasher's brain to waltz! I began to read "Mailer's America" with great interest. *Time* was inspired to reprint choice bits from *Miami and the Siege of Chicago*. Mailer's comments about Nixon and Humphrey (by the time you read this, the name of the next White Father Bird will be on the tip of your red, white, and blue tongue) were pretty good. His description of McCarthy's followers: "Their common denominator seemed to be found in some blank area of the soul, a species of disinfected idealism which gave one the impression when among them of living in a lobotomized ward of Upper Utopia."

Like the overture of true love which will last until dawn or until you have brushed your teeth, Mailer's comments got better. Naturally, his comment on civil rights and blacks interested the dishwasher: ". . . he was getting tired of Negroes and their rights. It was a miserable recognition, and on many a count, for if he felt even a hint this way, then what immeasurable tides of rage must be loose in America itself? . . . But he was so heartily sick listening to the tyranny of soul music, so bored with Negroes triumphantly late for appointments, so depressed with Black inhumanity to Black in Biafra, so weary of being sounded in the subway by black eyes, so despairing of the smell of booze and pot and used-up hope in blood-shot eyes of Negroes bombed at noon, so envious finally of that liberty to abdicate from the long year-end decade-drowning yokes of work and responsibility that he must have become in some secret part of his flesh a closet republican. . . ." Does personal despair, aging, the general mood of the times make a writer from the avant-garde uptight? Or was this "simple emotion" caused by the Reverend Abernathy's late appointment? Was Mailer looking for a fight? Years ago, he had written the famous *The White Negro*. He was the Father of Hip. He had almost single-handedly brought the world of Paul Bowles to the new frontier, exposing that world to thousands of middle-class youth and their elders. Certainly he had paid his slumming dues. Pot, pills, booze are old joys and night-mares to him—for he had touched the outer limits of despair in more than one instance. Even with his educa-tion, affluence, he went under in the dream, got flogged by the bats of hell. What could he possibly expect from American blacks in their situation? And now: "They had been a damned minority for too long, a huge in-digestible boulder in the voluminous, ruminating gov-ernment gut of every cowlike Democratic Administra-tion. Perhaps the WASP had to come to power in order that he grow up, in order that he take the old primitive root of his life-giving philosophy—which required every man to go through battles, if the world would live, and every woman to bear a child—yes, take that root off the high attic shelf of some Prudie Parsely of a witch—ancestor, and plant it in the smashed glass and burned brick of the 20th century's junkyard."

Prudie Parsely might have been incognito during the grass-green Eisenhower years. Indeed. But as I hunt and peck and go to press, Prudie has taken root and is trying to strangle anyone who opposes her. For years she has been the little sweet pea in the jolly green giant's pod; her small-town American heart (which is shaped exactly like a Norman Rockwell valentine) pulsed with security, a Dow Jones high of righteousness. Prudie was safe. Old Glory flew high, and God blessed the foreign descendants, and for a very long time they believed this was true. Heart of hearts! Vietnam, taxes, and black power made the beat irregular. Miss Parsely is aghast. She's a little afraid and is now working her army overtime. Anything goes. Why, the lady will take anything with two or four feet. Indeed. The little uptight white Protestants and their non-Protestant followers are getting it together. Whips sing in the air; blacks beware. Genocide, masquerading as Law and Order awaits you. So be prepared, pray that you take one and, hopefully, a hundred with you.

Just about the time you think everything is breaking even—even-steven, mail arrives. There is no escape. A survey questionnaire: "Why You Did or Did Not Sell Out to the Establishment." Among the men and women listed: Norman Mailer, Paul Getty, Frank Sinatra, Nina Simone, and Charles Wright. The dishwasher was amused. What tony company. A shot glass of amusement, I thought, and then made it down the hill, down to Harrison's. The lower-echelon employees were not allowed to drink in the hotel bar. Harrison's was the only bar for miles around—a typical highway bar—

these bars might well serve as a symbol of America; there was something magnificently expansive about them, yet they could suck in their breath, hold it, forever. Harrison's was located in the middle of the Catskills, and I had been mistaken for a Puerto Rican by a small-town Wasp who puked drunken black hatred. Another small-town Wasp offered to buy me drinks, then informed me that Governor Wallace would shortly appear on the television screen.

However, the mood of Harrison's that afternoon had the camaraderie of a late-summer afternoon. The television was turned off, and I ordered a double Scotch (I had received a small royalty check) which meant I would not have to signal the bartender-owner, who was reading John Updike's *Couples*.

"Chuck, my man," Chuck exclaimed. He was playing pool. Black, twenty-seven years old, he appeared to be extremely well adjusted. Chuck was the second cook at the hotel, and everyone liked him. Before making his last winning shot, he looked over at Miss Mary and winked. Miss Mary, as everyone called her, was a maid at the hotel and was something of a legend. Miss Mary owned a brand-new robin's-egg-blue Cadillac. Miss Mary was a moonlighter. I looked across at her, laughing over a Seagram and 7-Up with a couple of transient rednecks. Perhaps it was true, but I wouldn't fork over ten dollars or twenty dollars to Miss Mary. She was too much woman for me. But even after I turned away, the image of her tits under the white nylon uniform stayed with me. Those tits seemed capable of guiding an ocean liner into harbor. I wasn't interested in Miss Mary's face, although it was attractive, unlined. She must have been at least forty-five.

Chuck won, and there were a lot of bravos. He left with Miss Mary, left in his yellow Thunderbird.

The Thunderbird's motor was souped up, and I heard it as Chuck zoomed up the hill. I ordered another double, feeling a little down, wanting a little loving. Then I ordered a six-pack and made it.

About an hour later, there was a knock on my door.

"Chuck," Chuck said. "Busy, man?"

"No." I yawned through the door. "Come on in. The door's open."

Chuck entered in his dazzling cook's whites. His dazzling boyish smile was wide. We were never buddy-buddy but got along well.

"Oh, man. I'm sorry. You're reading. You gotta let me read some of your books."

"Any time," I said, sitting up. "Wanna beer?"

"Sure could use one. Hot as hell this afternoon. Must have put away two six-packs in the kitchen this afternoon."

"Yeah." I grinned. "That kitchen is a bitch."

"You read a lot," Chuck was saying, "and I'm sorry

to disturb you, but I came up to ask if you wanted a piece of ass."

This is just too goddamn much, I told myself. What's the angle? But already Junior was standing tall, waiting for me to put on my racing shoes.

"It's just down the hill," Chuck said. He wasn't looking at me then with that dazzling smile.

I stood up. "Anybody I know?"

"Yeah, man. Great piece of ass."

"Let's make it, baby."

"Man, you're ready," Chuck said as we made it down the hill. I kept on putting Junior in place, but the son of a bitch wanted to stand up and cheer.

The low-slung maids' quarters was a former chicken coop. Remodeling gave it the appearance of a jerry-built post-World-War II ranch house. Hundreds of stamping feet had killed the grass around the quarters. But the hardy hollyhocks survived; they grew tall; their riotous colors were like a torch against the surrounding countryside, and all was quiet except for the distant sound of B. B. King on a phonograph or a radio within the quarters.

Chuck, grinning, unlocked number 7; there must have been at least twenty keys on his chain, and they jingled like Oriental chimes.

"Well," he said, "here we are."

We walked directly into the living room, wallpapered

with an intricate design of garden flowers. Crepe-paper flowers were everywhere, plus the scent of lilac room refresher. For a moment, I thought I would pass out.

Chuck offered me a drink. "Mary made all of the flowers," he said with the sweet charm of an ambitious young mortician.

Muffling a laugh, I nodded. What was Chuck's game? Already, I was getting a little uneasy. Boredom had touched me on the shoulder.

"Want another drink?"

"Nope."

"Okay." Chuck sighed. "Mary's in the next room."

Miss Mary lay on the wide pastel-covered bed, her body (the color of muddy water) was voluptuous. What appeared to be a long curly wig outlined her pleasant face. She was wearing nothing but a strong support- ing white bra. I had never seen one like it, except on models in magazines. All the women I knew used little skinny bras.

Miss Mary had her eyes closed. A permanent smile colored her lips. I had a funny idea that Miss Mary might scream, and that her red lips might leap from her face and run out of the room.

"Hello, Chuck," Miss Mary said painfully.

"Hi," I chuckled. There was no door between the two rooms, and I could see Chuck sitting on the sofa. But he was not staring out the window. He was looking straight ahead at the floral papered walls. Junior was at parade rest, Miss Mary weighed at least 180. But what the hell! I stripped and sat down on the bed. Even after my hot hands touched her thighs, Junior was still at parade rest. I thought that Junior was retreating from the battlefield and told myself, Baby, you got your work cut out for you.

Miss Mary opened her eyes briefly and touched my arm. "It's all right," she said.

I didn't answer her. My hot, greedy hands reached for the bra. Miss Mary's hand had engulfed Junior, who still seemed in the act of retreating.

Good God! There must have been twenty goddamn hooks on the bra. My short arms could not encircle Miss Mary. Besides, she was trying to rise and anoint Junior, who was beginning to march.

"Wait a minute," I said. Miss Mary appeared not to hear me. She had raised up, opened her mouth, was prepared to sing to Junior. He was at attention, and I had the bra off. Junior stood firmly at attention as Miss Mary lovingly caressed him, but depression touched my shoulder. I didn't particularly want to get blown. But I lay back on the bed and let Mary work out. There was nothing extraordinary about her tongue and lips. I raised up and grabbed her tits—mini-blimps; a man could fly high and safe between them or, buoyed by their softness, sleep the sleep of rapture. I pulled Miss Mary up toward me. Now she was crying softly. She held on to Junior as if she wanted to squeeze the breath out of him.

Miss Mary wanted to baptize Junior again in the name of desire; I wanted to get laid.

"Come on," I said.

Miss Mary was breathing very hard. She had a coughing spell, but I went ahead, while the woman who made crepe-paper flowers protested. Desire had reached its peak with me. All I wanted was to plow into those 180 pounds.

"Chuck—Chuckie, please. Oh, no—"

But it was pleasant with the pillow under her. Yes, lovely, for although she was a large woman, a baby cantaloupe couldn't fit into her vagina. It didn't take very long. Spent, happy, and grinning, I tried to pull away.

"No," Miss Mary cried. Her large sweating body shook, and the most terrible sounds I had ever heard, fast and painful, seemed to come from her stomach. Junior was getting uneasy, and Miss Mary's arms had me in a bind.

I took her again, took her slow and easy—this one was for her and the flowers. Those terrible sounds had stopped, and I could feel her pleasure as her body moved toward me.

Grind, slow and easy. Her face in my hands, her

tongue in my mouth like a goldfish on a cake of ice, then suddenly she became rigid as her tongue sought mine and moans crept up from her throat.

"Don't get up," Miss Mary said.

I tried not to show my irritation. Leaning over, I kissed and caressed those fantastic tits. Oh! If Rubens were alive and I were a billionaire—I'd commission him to paint Miss Mary. The large, muddy-water-colored body against the pastel sheets and pillowcases, trimmed with lace (no doubt Miss Mary's personal touch), and masses of crepe-paper flowers that never grew in Mother Nature's garden. Henry Moore could do the boobs in bronze—what a bedside trophy.

"Chuckie," Miss Mary whined.

"Love, I've got to go to the bathroom."

I passed Chuck in the living room. "Okay, man?" He grinned.

Returning the grin, I said, "Right on, man."

It was a very humid afternoon, and I had planned to shower. But I wanted to lay Miss Mary again, plow into those 180 pounds. I hosed down Junior and the surrounding hairy pond, made my swift exit, whistling— are you ready? whistling, "Wish I were in Dixie again." Miss Mary was a pretty good lay, and I felt good.

In the living room, I drank from the Seagram quart bottle, then started toward the bedroom.

Chuck, finally clothed in the cook's whites, was on the

bed. I watched as he pulled Miss Mary's legs apart. She had her eyes closed and moaned like an old female cat. There was something ritualistic about their movements. Something familiar, and I didn't like it.

Chuck caressed the back-breaking large legs.

"Oh, Mama," he moaned. Then buried his head between Miss Mary's legs as if to sleep. Of course he did not sleep. A seemingly well-adjusted young man with a neat Afro crew cut, his medium-sized head became a spinning top. Several times he jerked his head back and stared into Miss Mary's door of life, before diving back down. Miss Mary's legs rested on Chuck's slender shoulders. There was something crude about her movements as she pressed Chuck's head tighter. But the young, black second cook was balling. Apparently, he preferred the leftover juices from our luncheon.

Nathanael West
First Comfort Station
Purgatorial Heights

Dear West:

Por favor—forgive the delay. True, it has been almost six years. Hope that it has been less than a day in your particular hell. It began in our New York and followed me through the small transient rooms of all your depressing hotels. Now Absurdity and Truth pave the parquet of my mind. The pain is akin to raw alcohol on the testicles. But I'm not complaining. Life's eyedropper is being sterilized with ant piss. Hallucinations? Joshing? West—I-Am-Not-Spaced-Out, despite the East and West Village rumors. Slightly skulled though. Celebrating the Day of the Dead.

I suppose the dead dog at the bottom of Malcolm Lowry's Mexican ravine is almost home now. But the yellow-button white daisies have taken root. I like that.

Take care and watch the shit.

Charles

P.S. Here's a little clipping from *The New York Times:* "Aosta, Italy (AP)—Cold, avalanches, and lack of food killed about 20 percent of the wild Alpine goats and chamois in Grand Paradise."